SHOCKING CIRCUMSTANCES

SHOCKING CIRCUMSTANCES

Book I
LAST SHINE

Chris Roy

NEW PULP PRESS

Published by New Pulp Press, LLC, 926 Truman Avenue, Key West, Florida 33040, USA.

For information contact:
Publisher@NewPulpPress.com

Printed in the United States of America
Visit us on the web at www.newpulppress.com

ISBN-13: 978-1945734076 (New Pulp Press)
ISBN-10: 1945734078

For my wife, Melanie Jean, whose courage, loyalty and beauty give me reason to hope and accomplish.

"Fights are not won in the ring; they are won in the gym, in preparation."

-Fred Williams

SHOCKING CIRCUMSTANCES

PART I

THE GUN smacked into the man's face with a sound only solid metal hitting flesh can make. An arch of pink sweat glistened briefly in a ray of sunlight before sticking to a shadowed wall.

The man's head rolled around his shoulders, eyes showing whites, his mouth burbling incoherently. A garden hose was pointed at the man, turned on, spraying him in the face. He moaned, rolling his head around again to move his mouth and nose clear of the water.

A second assailant stepped forward with a small Taser in his hand. Stuck it to the man's neck. Jolted him with a low current, zapping him back to consciousness.

A loud slap resonated throughout the building. "Tell me where it is, Jose. Where did you hide it?"

The slap again. "I will beat you to a slow death, you know that? I will saw off your fucking balls. WHERE'S THE GODDAMN MONEY?" demanded a man of enormous girth. Tall and pale with a hair-trigger temper, his face was unremittingly red, his breath an incessant wheeze. He slapped Jose with a hand as big as a catcher's mitt. "Where is it?!" he shouted with spittle on his lips, veins in his neck and forehead bulging, turning his skin shades of red into purple.

"Jose, come on, *amigo*. You don't have to go through this. Just tell us, okay? *Dónde esta?*" the partner pleaded, playing his natural role as the Good Guy. He really believed he was a good guy. Doing what needed to be done so that he

1

could take care of his family, watch his partner's back. Though the term "good" was taken to a new level today, he thought. He fidgeted, his fireplug body and chubby Latin face filled with worry.

The place stank of mildew, rotten wood. Of blood and sweat. Of fear. Odors that imbibe paranoia. Hector was constantly looking over his shoulder, listening to the silence of the building and the lack of wind or natural noises from outside.

It was unsettling.

A train horn sounded from miles away, seeming to crescendo inside the death shrouded room, causing Hector to jump and curse a string of Spanish. He breathed deeply to slow his heartbeat. Tried to focus on the job at hand.

Jose gurgled and choked, coughed to clear his throat. Caught his breath. He lifted his head and glared at his enemies. "*Cabrones*," he spat. "La Familia has shown you loyalty. Has taken care of you. And you show your gratitude with betrayal? Goat fucking pigs! The worst kind of traitors." He tensed in pain, struggling to overcome it and continue talking. "I was only mildly surprised by your treachery, *gordo*," he said to the huge white man, then spat blood at him. His eyes moved to the other man. "But you, Hector. You are Mexicano, with roots in Juarez. The cartel is your blood. This betrayal will crush your family. They will be exterminated like cockroaches." He spat again and glared to emphasize his words.

Jimmy wasn't impressed. He stepped forward, grunting with the effort as he threw a fist into Jose's stomach. The thud knocked the wind from him, expelled breath thickening the air with more blood and sweat. The ropes holding Jose to the chair strained as his body tried to double over from the pain.

"Where is it? WHERE THE FUCK IS THE MONEY?!" Jimmy shouted in rage, shaking with something far beyond impatience. He screamed and started throwing punch after punch into Jose's face, stomach, and ribs, his gloved fists dishing out bruises and fractures with every blow. The abandoned apartment building echoed with the fury, but its filthy walls, trash-strewn floors and busted windows were unconcerned witnesses to the brutality.

Jimmy stooped with both hands on his knees. Bent over and wheezing like he was the one being assaulted. He looked over at his partner. "Hose...Him...Taser," he gasped.

Hector grabbed the hose and twisted the nozzle. The cold stream of water revived Jose enough so that he didn't have to use the modified Taser. "I don't think this was a good idea, Jimmy," he said, turning the hose off. "He's not going to talk. Jose didn't get to be a lieutenant by being weak."

"What, are you scared now? Getting a conscience all of a sudden? It's too late for that. We can't just quit and let him go." He paused and looked at his partner and only friend. "Look, these greasy motherfuckers owe us, Hector. Everybody owes us, this entire community. We have served the public on these ungrateful streets for ten years, saving lives and sending the trash to prison. And what do we have to show for it? An anorexic bank account and more time on the goddamn streets! They owe us, and so does this trash right here," he said, pushing a tree branch-like finger into Jose's forehead. "He owes us for not putting him away years ago." His face poured sweat, unhealthy with dark red splotches on pallid skin, eyes enormous with lack of circulation and a touch of insanity.

He spun back to Jose, who was laughing.

"Hector is right, Jimmy," Jose croaked, still laughing. His slight frame shook in his yellow silk shirt, eyes alight with the antagonizing desire he felt towards the man he knew would kill him. "And you are wrong in your justification. There is no just due. Nobody owes you. It is greed that controls your life now." His teeth showed in a bloody smile. "It's greed that has sentenced you to death."

Grunting ferociously, Jimmy reared back and slapped him again, putting his whole body into the swing, knocking the chair over backwards. Jose's body slammed on the floor, thumping his head on the hard, filthy tile. Jimmy leaned down and grabbed his shoulders, pulled up, setting the chair upright again.

He growled in Jose's face. "Now, you listen to me, big shot, big shit, mafia wannabe greaser." His voice dropped to an ominous whisper. "You are nothing now. Nothing," he breathed hotly. "You have been screwing me out of my money for three years, and now it's my turn to do the screwing." He smiled pleasantly. "You know, we learned quite a bit about serial killers and their various torture methods at the academy. I would love to try out a few of my favorites on you. You will suffer in pain beyond comprehension. I'll give you blood transfusions and bring you back to life with a fucking defibrillator so I can kill you and revive you again and again. And again." Another smile. "But it doesn't have to be that way. Tell me where you hid the money and I'll end it quick and clean, right now." He snapped his fingers.

Jose whispered like he wasn't strong enough to speak. He grunted with a swing of his head, motioning Jimmy to come closer. Jimmy leaned down with his ear to Jose's mouth. "*Chinga tu madre*," he said, then spat blood on the side of Jimmy's face.

"You're dead! You're fucking dead, greaser!" Jimmy flustered in anger, then thundered his fists into Jose's face once more, wheezing and missing as he tired. After eight punches, he ran out of breath and fell on one knee, gasping loudly.

Jose managed to laugh through the final barrage, laughing even harder when he quit. "No, fat man Jimmy. It is you who are dead. Traitors are stupid by definition, and always make mistakes." He coughed, blood ran out of his mouth and down his clean-shaven chin and neck. His diehard manner and righteous final words would honor his Aztec warrior ancestry. "If my *hermanos* don't avenge me, someone else will get you. Sooner, rather than later."

Jimmy lost all reason and rational thought. Face purple and bellowing between breaths, he drew his gun and shot Jose in his face from where he knelt. The .40 Black Talon entered at his chin and went through his mouth and out the back of his neck, severing the spinal cord and traveling through two sheetrock walls before lodging in a wooden stud. The explosion of his head was graphic, like a hot pocket left in the microwave for too long, popping on one end, spraying sauce in all directions. The wall and floor behind him were covered in bits of bone, blood, gray matter, chunks of hair and skin. Pigeons cooed and flapped away from the open, busted windows, emptying their frightened bowels on the concrete and lawn below.

From the wall of gore an incisor fell free, hitting the floor tiles with a chink in the silent aftermath.

Hector gasped. "Oh, Jimmy. No! Not the Sig. Why did you use the Sig?" He stood with his hands gripping his hair, staring at what was left of Jose's face with horror. "This is bad, amigo. Really bad. You were supposed to use the .38, the throwaway. Not your issue!" he whined. Stressed out about Jose's threat to his family, dismay and conflict now completely ruled his mind with this new problem in the picture.

"Shut up, shut up! I know that. It's under control," Jimmy snarled. Having regained his breath and part of his composure, he realized the potential consequences of his mistake and made a serious effort to get his temper under control, to compose a new plan. "Don't worry about it. It was only one bullet. We'll take his head and throw it in the bayou. They'll never find it. Our cartel guys will think it was an MS-13 hit."

"Take his head? You want to take his head? *Madre de Dios*," he whined, then crossed himself.

"Yes. Listen to me, goddamn it. We needed to do this. This piece of shit was in our way. We talked about this. He's the reason our cut was only five percent. The ungrateful prick is out of the way now, so we'll get more money. Your family will get more money now. Let's stay focused on why we had to do this, Hector."

"All right, Jimmy. Let's hurry, okay? We have been here for way too long already."

Jimmy unsnapped his knife sheath and slid out his six-inch serrated Gerber blade. Grabbing Jose's hair with one hand, he sawed through the esophagus, muscles and tendons, then dug around and found a spot between two vertebrae to complete the severing. He didn't get what he had come for, and the dead eyes and death's head grin seemed to mock him for his failure. He growled unhappily.

"I found it, Jimmy," Hector called, relief evident in his voice as he walked from the hallway holding a deformed slug between two fingers. He stuck it in his pocket with a grimace. "It was stuck in a stud, in the back room. Got lucky, *ese*."

"Right. Good. The crime scene unit won't have a bullet or a head to find out what kind of bullet was used. But they could find our hair, prints, or something. We'll have to burn the place. That'll clean it up. Do you have a lighter?" he asked, knowing his partner sometimes smoked.

"Yeah, Jimmy. I'll make a fire. Let's just go, okay? I'm getting spooked."

"All right, all right! We're going. Don't start that Mexican spirits of the dead crap again. This is one greaser that won't be haunting us, I promise you. He'll be haunting some stinking bayou in about fifteen minutes."

"Whatever you say, Jimmy."

Hector shook his head and walked back down the hallway, stepping over an Arby's bag with holes chewed in it, stopping where he had earlier found a jug of paint thinner. He picked up the container, wondering if someone had abandoned it along with their plans to restore the apartment. The entire neighborhood had deserted the area, unable to afford to rebuild after Hurricane Katrina had caused the building codes to change. The police kept out squatters and junkies very effectively.

And the officers that made that extra effort are the same ones that used this neighborhood for their personal affairs, he just realized. He shook his head again.

"Well, no one will use this place again. Sheesh. What have you gotten yourself into, Hector?" he muttered to himself, unscrewing the cap. He poured the mineral spirits all over the floor and walls. Walked the liquid trail down the hall and into the front room with Jose. He splashed it around the body but couldn't quite bring himself to throw it on the cartel lieutenant. Squatting down, he struck his lighter and the room slowly bloomed with firelight.

Walking outside, Hector saw Jimmy rummaging through Jose's car, a new champagne colored BMW M3. The glass had been recently cleaned and reflected a morning sky that seemed supernaturally clear and pure in contrast to the street below. The yard was a trashed clone of the other lots on the abandoned street, overgrown with weeds and littered with fast food packages, old, rusted kitchen appliances, and diapers. It was diseased. Clusters of pox on hairy, filthy skin. The apartment buildings were mere skeletons of their pre-Katrina glory, gutted and ugly with stripped paint and rotten wood that could be sensed every time a breeze drifted through.

The scene matched Hector's mood, compounding it.

Maybe a fire is what this place really needs, he reasoned,

looking around and envisioning an inferno consuming the filth and corruption. "We are going to burn for our corruption one day, too," he prophesied to the neighborhood.

"What?" Jimmy yelled, still digging around in the car.

"I lit the fire."

"Good. Set this car on fire, too. There's nothing in it worth anything. Dammit!" He threw down some papers and slammed the center console shut. Got out, looked Hector in the eye. "I wish I could bring the bastard back to life so I could kill him again. They owe us, Hector. They fucking owe us!"

Kill him again? Hopefully you'll use the .38 next time, Hector thought to himself. He didn't say anything, knowing that continuing to talk about the money they didn't get would only make the situation worse. And, he discovered, he was scared to say anything. Scared of the person his partner had become.

He popped the hood on the BMW and used his knife to cut a fuel line. Then he walked back to the driver's side and turned the key on. The fuel pump cycled on and off to prime the engine, spraying gasoline all over the engine compartment and ground. He turned the key off, then on again to spray more fuel. Then, he squatted down and struck his lighter.

The car burst into flames.

"Let's go, Hector. We have to dispose of this son of a bitch's head and get back to work." Jimmy got into their car, closed the door.

"Yeah. Let's get back to work," he replied, adjusting his uniform back into regulatory position. For a moment he stood there, studying the side of their patrol car, noticing how the name of the place he once swore to protect and serve mocked him in return. *City of Biloxi Police*, its bold, black presence stood out in sharp contrast against the pristine white of the front and rear door panels. The dark letters seeping in and scarring the rest of the sanctified body, abusing their place of honor much like the two men who rode inside.

He fell into the passenger seat with a defeated slump, closed the door behind him, and sighed. Flames from the BMW's carcass danced like victorious, evil spirits across the cruiser's mirrored surface, echoing their laughter along the right side of Hector's sullen face as they drove away from the scene.

He dug a pack of Winston's from his uniform pocket and placed a crooked cigarette between two nervous fingers. Turning slightly so as not to arouse Jimmy's suspicion, he crossed himself anxiously, resigning himself to the chaos ahead.

PART II

Ocean Springs – Gautier, Mississippi
March 17, 2010

"I'M NOT doing it, Silvio. I'm done. I'm not the Shocker anymore."

He groaned, lowered his voice. I pictured him turning away from the press guys. "I've already sold it to them. They expect it. You know this is the meal ticket. The money shot, baby. It could only hurt the promotion if you don't do it now. We gotta get with the program here."

"News flash, Silvio: there is no program. It's my last fight. I don't care if I ever sell another ticket or pay-per-view buy again. And Hopkins will do that this card, anyway. He's the main event." My mind was still able to argue the issue, but my body was screaming, Shut up you dumbass. I want my button pushed!

"Hang on, Shock. One minute," he said sourly. He put his hand over the phone and engaged his media associates in a rapid-fire negotiation, tones muffled. I couldn't understand a word.

Dammit.

I considered making fun of him for not knowing how to push the mute button.

Approaching the end of the beautiful bridge, I told myself I should turn around, go find another track to run. Maybe this bridge. It had a pedestrian lane and some major incline/decline work for whoever bounced their boobs on its concrete. Plus the view. Incredible.

The morning sun raked the waves, turning them a golden blue. The ripples looked small from up here but were probably rocking the hell out of those little fishing boats and pleasure crafts down in the channel. The salty breeze was perfect, not too cool for a pre-spring a.m.

The daydream ended with me looking around downtown Ocean Springs. The intersection of Washington Avenue and Highway 90 looked impossibly busy for such a small town. Where the heck did all these people come from? I continued driving east, lazily shifting the El Camino's Tremec five-speed, popping the clutch just a little too fast for second gear.

Chirp! my tires beckoned.

I grinned and squirmed in my seat. Man, that sound, that hint of the power at my command, made me so hot. Made me tingle and sweat and giggle in anticipation of a long stretch of road I could gun him on.

Yes, him. Camino was a man who knew how to treat a girl. And this girl was hot in the ass for him. I mean, next time someone asks how I stay so trim, I'm gonna point at Camino. Forget the hours of boxing cardio every day. Jump in this baby and have your metabolic rate spike through the roof.

Hot.

I revved it and chirped third. Ooh, couldn't help myself.

Submitting to my weak will today, I sighed and hung a right off the highway, passed some grease pit grill and low budget motel, turned left into the stadium parking area. My body wanted its button pushed, and I was too much of a sissy to deny it

The Rush Button. The itch was beginning to turn into an ache.

I still had the phone to my ear. I screamed a few times to get Silvio's attention.

"What's that, Shock?"

"I'm here, man. Might as well do it," I said a tad too sharply.

Say one thing, do another. I hate it when that happens. I could hear Silvio's smug smile and his thoughts on female stereotypes.

"Great! Look, Shocker. Forget about it, right? Just do your thing. I'll try to get you some extras for your kid and hubby."

He meant Sports Illustrated or The Ring t-shirts, cups and crap. Didn't need it. Didn't want it in my house. But my family did, and I always compromised for that reason.

I said, "Sure. Whatever. But no swimsuit stuff. I already caught Nolan watching porn. I'm not ready to deal with that yet."

I ended the call, parked my ride about sixty yards from Silvio's Lincoln Navigator and the two ugly blue Ford Taurus rentals clustered next to it. I needed to give them a stage to film, an act I've done many times. Too many.

Looking at the iPhone in my lap, I thumbed it, scrolled to memos to jot a note about shock therapy, planning to Google it later. Thought about it for a second, then added addiction as a hit word. Could be some research from those old psych sessions that'll be of interest to me. I wasn't proud of this shit. It was the only vice I had. Well, unless you count swearing. And knocking women out (when I could have just out-boxed them). Sometimes I swear while I'm knocking them out. Combining the two is much more gratifying.

On reflection, shock addiction should be the least of my worries.

What's your opinion?

I dropped the phone on the passenger seat. Looked out the windshield and studied the Ocean Springs Greyhound's stadium. A normal high school football set up, nice and clean, what was expected of a town with a large portion of middle-class wealth.

The track circling the field was a standard four-hundred meter deal. And my bitch. I make any track my bitch.

After I get my dose, anyway. Let's do it.

I stepped out of Camino. My self-awareness, like any decent performer, told me what the media sees and how to act accordingly. I'm a Fifty Yard Girl. You know, a girl that looks gorgeous from fifty yards away. Super fit body with curves and silk-shiny hair that convinces you I'm a Ten from a distance. Then you get up close and see that I'm a Butterface. You know, everything looks good but-her-face. I was white, but not too white. I ran outside almost every day and that gave me a nice tone. But that doesn't make my Miss Piggy nose look any sexier. Or the laugh lines that spiraled off the corners of my eyes and lips and would look more natural on a forty-year-old Everlast bag.

Maybe that's a little harsh.

But my body is a masterpiece, a finely tuned and toned machine. I'm so proud of it. Probably why I have the laugh lines. Legs and butt like a black girl, though I have no clue how that happened, considering my Greek and German heredity. Who keeps up with that lineage crap anymore?

And I'm fast. As The Ring printed it, I'm "ultra-fast." My speed has enabled me to beat fighters that were favored to win, women with more ring experience and skills. Most people are skeptical when hearing of my ability, assuming that the tales are exaggerated. And I prefer it that way; they never see me coming. Literally.

My blue Umbro shorts were a thin material that fluttered and clung to my curves nicely, showing superior conditioned thighs and my tiny size two waist. And wonderful ass. If a genie appeared and offered to give me a pretty face in exchange for my great glutes, I'd tell him to go magically fuck himself. I'd choose to rock the booty.

Up top I didn't have much to brag about. I had a pink Under Armor running tank top, so cute, hugging my B-cups and showing the faint outline of a thick sports bra. The bra was an important training component. Even small boobs flop around, and after a while, hurt like a bastard.

I popped the hood by pulling the lever under the dash. Left the engine running. Stood and put a hand to my mouth, yawning. All an act. I'm a tired, average Jane, dragging around early in the morning. I walked to the front of the truck, again with the presence of mind to picture what they see. A gleaming red and gray hot rod, long fins along the bedrails, ending with custom LED lights. Polished aluminum, twenty-inch wheels twinkling like chrome, wicked blade designs with low-profile tires. Monster engine idle-loping its beastly growl in the still, cool air. Smoking hot athletic chick standing between the headlights and popping the latch under the hood.

Eye candy for a muscle car ad. Can you dig it?

I opened the engine compartment and smiled at the Snarling Darling inside. A 427 CID big block with 580 HP. Built it myself about four years ago, especially for Camino. I stared at the MSD Blaster II ignition coil and my heart started galloping against my sports bra.

Crap.

The coil was my pipe. My needle. And there wasn't a single day that I didn't wake up thinking about it.

Could be a problem? It was a ginormous fucking problem!

I shouldn't do this. But I wanted to. Did I need to? Nah. I could do it. Maybe just half a hit... Make up your mind!

"Christ," I muttered, then chuckled. "Half a hit? Really, Clarice?"

I took a big whiff of the lovely mélange of hot engine odors, then grabbed the coil wire and popped the rubber grommet off the coil. The tiny bolt of lightning clicked its twenty thousand volts brightly through the gap, arching like the current was electric whips snapping to show off the power hidden within. The engine stuttered like it was out of breath. I guess it was. I glanced at Silvio and he nodded his head energetically. His hands were stuck out like he was doing double Karate chops, or something.

Still I hesitated. I looked at the track and thought of the run, the sharp feeling of excitement from going so fast under my own power, knocking out three miles in seventeen minutes flat. The weather was perfect for it. Sixty degrees at sea level, clear sky. Best conditions for athletic performance. I looked back at the Snarling Darling, thinking how odd it was that it ran at its best in these conditions, too, sharing a major performance trait with humans. Remembering that usually made me want to bond with Camino, take him to his limits on days I take myself to my limits. We both get a workout.

Bonding. How many ways have I bonded with this machine? Some say I am a machine.

I say, Watch me.

I stuck my hand in the lightning. And suddenly, I wasn't the sleepy, dragging ass girl anymore. I was a rip-snort bellowing monster, a supercharged engine with incalculable horsepower. I acted out my role without acting. When twenty thousand volts takes a bite out of your spinal cord, you aren't capable of acting.

The engine died. But I was so ALIVE. It felt like my hair was sticking straight up, long dark brown spikes of energized Paul Mitchell products. But it was in a ponytail. I think. My hazel eyes were blurred, emotional, overjoyed with the flowing sensation of raw power.

I yelled again and did a chest flex, jumped in the air several times, sucking in deep breaths to get some extra oxygen in to fuel my fire. A few more red counts to where it's all happening upstairs.

Sufficiently hyped and unable to just stand there, I took off running. My black and pink Nike Shox were probably happy I was so light because I tried my damndest to thrust and pound and burn the motherfuckers up in a blur on takeoff. At speed, they barely touched the asphalt as I sprinted toward the chain-link fence that encompassed the football field. I vaulted it like it wasn't there, nothing to it, and heard Silvio whoop out a cheer that resounded throughout the empty stadium. I hit the track and set a pace that my inner clock said would make a mile in six minutes, at 10 MPH. I'd run eight laps at that speed, two miles, then pick it up a step and make the third mile in five.

Twelve laps total. No prob.

My system was really pumping from the coil shock. In my mind's eye, I could see the twenty-thousand volts entering at my hand and being conducted throughout my body at near the speed of light, overwhelming the far lesser biological impulses my nervous system sputtered out, supercharging my cardiac nerve, racing through my arms, legs and brain stem, orchestrating hormones and neurotransmitters any ol' damn way it pleased.

Blaster II power, baby. Cerebral Blaster. I should start manufacturing my own coils with that brand. Boss hog in any car and any body.

My racing heart took center stage in my consciousness, beating like an 808 drum, rhythmic, solid. Strong. Not the racing of fatigue or from cortisol saturation. It pounded with that Good Vibration that comes from only one source.

Premium fuel, yo.

Oh, the do-me-do-me-do-me-do-me racing of adrenaline, pure and clean. I couldn't get any more if I were chewing on adrenal glands.

I knocked out half my run in my own wacky world, cruising through planet Performance, where anything is possible and there are no limits. Then I remembered the media dogs were trackside, at the designated Start/Finish line, snapping photos and commentating videos. The usual B.S. about my form, how smooth I was, legs kicking high, elbows thrusting back. Head up and breasts out to expand the diaphragm, blah, blah, blah. They'll make clever quips on my eccentric method of prepping for a workout. No coffee for this girl! they'll say. She goes for the real jumper cables. A few words to include my Shox in the job, and voila. Publicity antics to rival the hookers in pro wrestling.

As I rounded a curve, I thought about how much fun it would be to beat up a WWE Diva. Show everybody they were phonies. Would that be awesome, or what?

If you're thinking I'm jealous or a hater, or whatever, you're right. They make more money than me. And for playing.

Freaking panties fights? Come on.

Last mile. Gotta shake my rump a step faster. Stretch those legs out. Ooh, that feels so good. The endorphins were really hammering me, seducing me, tricking me into thinking my muscles fibers were not being torn and abused but wanted more power applied. More fuel in the carburetor.

Well, why the hell not?

The quiet stadium echoed with a soft, rapid tapping as my shoes thrust me around the curved lines of the track. The tapping increased in pace, but at the same time became fainter because my heels no longer hit. Only my toes were striking the surface, like a caress, with a finesse that comes from years of running experience. Ten years, six days a week. Eight years as a pro.

Yep. Mamma has some miles on her piggies.

Last lap. I sprinted around the final curve and saw that The Ring guy, a slim Latino dude of about thirty, was looking at a stopwatch. I ran as hard as I could, eking out a burst of reserved juice to blast over the Finish line. Slowed, walked. Fiended for a drink of water.

Silvio jogged up to me. "Very nice, Shocker. Very nice," he said, handing me a Gatorade lemon ice drink bottle. I snatched it and glared at him. It was my favorite, and I couldn't drink it. The cold, wet bottle soaked my hand with relief, teasing, promising more of that same alleviating bliss for the rest of my body.

I wanted to slap Silvio.

"Did you see," I panted, waiting for my mouth to unstick. "A cloud of dust on the track?"

"Say again?" he replied.

"My mouth feels like I just blew the animated-sand version of The Mummy. Dry, dammit."

"Er, I'm sorry?" he said, smiling at my charming grievance.

My throat clicked shut again and I thought it would never open. Talk about an uncomfortable feeling. Having to dehydrate several days before a weigh-in was torture. I twisted the cap off the bottle, squirted a stream of liquid ecstasy in my mouth, swished it around. I wanted to swallow it. Break the rules. The urge was on par with yearning for Camino's shock. I cheated a little, gulped a few ounces, spit out the rest. Very ladylike. A camera clicked, sounding like my Mummy-violated throat. I turned to look into the camera, gave a nice snarl and spat again.

Feeding the media machine. The antics usually suck. The pay usually makes up for it.

Usually.

The Ring guy walked with a digital audio recorder in his hand, pointing it at me. He smiled and looked professional enough, then fell weak to his baser needs and began glancing furtively at my legs. Looks of lust, not aesthetic admiration. Well, whatever. That's what I built the things for. Your lust is my power, dude.

He wore a t-shirt with a portrait of Old School fighters on the front. Ezzard Charles knocking Jersey Joe Walcott on his butt. To me, it looked comical on him. His too-effeminate, never-been-in-a-fight looks had one saving grace: a nice smile. I smiled back.

Get with the program, right?

"Clarice 'Shocker' Ares, your weigh-in is tomorrow. Are you going to make the one-hundred-and-eighteen pound limit?" he asked in an elite college prose, soft, no accent. He held the recorder deal closer to my face.

"I wouldn't be spitting out my favorite drink if I wasn't trying to," I responded, eyeing the Gatorade with exaggerated longing.

They all gave a courtesy laugh. Even though that shit wasn't funny. Hey, I'm their current gold mine. They've laughed at much sillier things I've said.

I abruptly quieted, looked at him seriously. "I was one-twenty before I came here. I figure after that run and making you hold up for that pugilist's t-shirt I should be pretty close."

He laughed like we were all sitting around a patio having over-priced tea, jesting one another. My mouth smiled but my eyes didn't. I made sure he noticed, then moved just a bit too fast to grab a towel Silvio was holding, causing the guy to flinch, thinking I was attacking him.

He stopped laughing. Silvio and the other journalist laughed harder. I sighed, feeling bad.

Silvio saw the intent on my face and stepped in front of me before I could apologize. He's the one that put me up to threatening these reporter-types on occasion. Supplements the whole crazy electrocution show, helps sell tickets, and, the best part for me, it makes for some entertaining reading. It was all fun and games until someone became terrorized and made me feel like a turd, though. I'm really a nice person.

My opponents would strongly disagree. But it's true. I promise.

The Latino journalist turned off his recorder and retreated to find his balls, glaring at everyone reproachfully, the poor thing. The Sports Illustrated guy walked up next to me, smiling at his colleague's withdrawal. He had a nice brown suit jacket on, no tie, white button-up deal and blue jeans, looking comfy. Sandy hair and a pencil mustache, late thirties. His eyes squinted from the sun rising behind me, which probably made a choice backdrop for the video he shot with a small HD camcorder in his left hand, his right stuffed carelessly in his jeans pocket.

"Impressive run, Ms. Ares," he said, as if commenting on a fine wine. "Have you ever run three miles in sixteen minutes, thirty-seven seconds?"

"I'm not sure. I really don't keep up with it. I just do my best, train hard to prepare for the fight." Downplay it, don't boast. They eat that crap up. Later, if he shows up at the fight, I'll have to threaten him, throw him off, make him write something to keep up the lunatic chick image the public loves. All very Tyson-esque.

Sixteen thirty-seven? I turned to look at the track, expecting it to be on fire.

I lit that mother' up!

"You are too modest," he continued, smiling. He had something in his teeth that looked gross. It was hard to keep a straight face. I tapped a fingernail to my teeth, looked from his eyes to his mouth. Didn't work. "Did the pre-run shock enhance your performance? Perhaps we should notify the Anti-Doping Agency and have them ban 'shock devices' as performance enhancing supplements."

Everyone laughed. That was a pretty good one, actually.

"You better not," I said, shaking a fist at him. "Those idiots might actually do it, then all of my fights would be suspect."

He asked several more questions to gauge my confidence for the upcoming bout, then I shook both of the journalists' hands and thanked them, ending the interview. Silvio caught my eye, jerked his head with meaning. I sighed and squeezed The Ring dude's hand a lot harder than was proper, winking at him. He jerked his hand back warily, turned and marched off, huffy.

Boy, I couldn't wait to read the next Ring issue. He'll surely have some juicy wild lady metaphors in there I can giggle over.

They jumped into their rental cars, and guess which one didn't wave as they drove past and turned toward the highway?

I looked at my promoter. Shrugged.

"That went very well. Very well," he said, rubbing his hands. The humongous gold band and yellow diamond on his pinky finger caught the sun and threw a golden laser in my eye. He must polish that ring religiously. Silvio looked superb in his blue Armani suit and calfskin shoes. He had the old style Italian fashioned hair, combed straight back with a light coating of grease. To make it shine and say, Fa'gettaboutit!

His over fifty face was naturally tan with few wrinkles, dark but cheerful eyes. Handsome guy. The image-ruining thing about the man was his stomach. It hung down where his junk is supposed to dwell, like he used to be five hundred pounds and lost three hundred of it. He's got a vault of money a Saudi prince would salivate over. He could get a tuck. Three-thousand dollar outfit, boss hair, and a hundred-dollar cigar in his be-ringed hand. All good. But the stomach drooping like that...

Guys. Please exercise and eat clean.

"How's the shoulder?" he said, a shadow of genuine concern crossing his face. Concern about me or his promotion, I'll never know. But it was genuine.

"Set it on fire two weeks ago doing pushups. Rotator cuff is really taxed. We put heat packs on it before workouts and ice it after. We'll manage it."

I say "we" as in my coach and I. We've been working the

crap out of my left-hook, too, and plan to use it as the money punch instead of my straight right. I told this to Silvio.

"Great idea, doll. Torres won't expect that. She'll be looking to avoid your right as you set up the hook. Brilliant."

"Thank Eddy."

"I will."

"We've studied the tapes on her last few fights and have a strategy that'll get the hook on the inside where we can do some damage. Could be a knockout first for my left."

"Be sure to say that at the pre-fight press conference tomorrow."

"No can do, chief. I never give away our fight plan, unlike the other fighters in your stable."

He frowned, hit a palm on his forehead. "Don't know what I was thinking. You're not an ego maniac like those other animals."

"Well..."

"Forget about it."

"Don't worry, Silvio. I'll be the Shocker at the conference. One last time, just for you."

"You're a doll. See you in Philly."

"We're on the plane tonight."

He shook my hand, patted my shoulder, got into his badass Navigator. I jumped into Camino after I had checked the coil wire. Silvio had re-plugged it and turned the key off. Routine teamwork.

Six years with this guy and we've had no major problems. My first promoter was a tool. A pimp that thought I was a prostitute he could sell at any venue he pleased. Negative. Cue game show loser buzzer. Eaaattt! Wrong answer, pal. When I finally got over my naïveté of the fight game – thanks to Eddy, my coach – I bucked his system. To teach me a lesson, he screwed me out of a purse on my sixth fight. It was my first five-digit purse. Receiving only four of the digits made me want to put a Ringside

Products t-shirt on him and work his ass like a heavy bag. But that would be even more illegal than what he did. And I always follow the rules.

But Eddy didn't.

Eddy wanted to get some payback, send a message so that the butthole would know who did it. The answer was obvious. So one night, Eddy broke into my promoter's little Audi and ran a wire from the ignition coil to the driver's seat. Stripped about a foot of the wire bare and splayed it over the seat cushion, fanning out the copper strands like thin tendrils on an exotic plant. A poisonous one. We hid behind an SUV in the parking lot and watched the greasy turd get in, close the door, start the engine and howl like a monkey under attack by a leopard.

Or something like that. Definitely an Animal Planet moment.

I laughed and ruined a great outfit rolling on the ground. I don't know what came over me, because I felt a strong urge to run over to him and scream, What's my name, bitch?! Eddy, laughing, had to hold me back.

The next day I met with my promoter to discuss our next venue. I mentioned "The Shocker" in the third person as many times as I could just to see him twitch every time I said it. Fun, but didn't give me the satisfaction I'd hoped for. I felt he deserved worse. Good thing for him revenge isn't my thing. I was raised by Christian parents who drilled me with morals and standards, etiquette, all the bells and whistles

But the prank worked. I mean, he obviously knew who cooked his cakes, but he didn't screw me anymore. Like he was a freshly tamed dog in a yard with an electric fence around the perimeter. And he knew if he was naughty and tired to go outside his boundary, he'd get stung again.

Good doggy.

I suffered another year of greasy deals until our

contract was up, then we split. And I was sooo glad, too, because I was feeling pretty darn amoral by that point. The guy made me not trust myself. I even bought a Ringside t-shirt in his size.

Smiling at the memory of that little creep in his Audi electric chair, I slid in and fired up the Snarling Darling, gracing my cakes on the suede seats. Gray suede. Matched the carpeting and door panels. The metal of the dash and doors was the same color red as the exterior. Groovy smooth.

Tssst ... Hot.

I was squirming before I even put it in gear.

I raced out onto the highway, stainless steel Borla mufflers roaring a deep, throaty challenge to everyone I passed. So I imagined, anyway. Made me feel gooo-d. Made me wiggle and giggle and believe I was possessed by a powerful sex god.

The husband was in trouble tonight, for sure. Yes, dear, he'll say. I'll give you as many Magic Os as you can handle.

Fan-fucking-tastic. I chirped third-gear.

~ ~ ~

That little run was merely a warm-up. The real fun was going down in this gym, Punchline. A fairly new joint off the highway in Gautier, a small town between Ocean Springs and Pascagoula. It was super nice. Too clean, according to my coach. He liked the old, battered establishments like you see in movies. Personally, I prefer the clean ones.

Punchline was owned and run by a splendid black dude named Ronald. This guy was definitely a tiger in his day. A very slick, very fast pro that kicked ass in the welter and junior middleweight divisions back in the '90s. He's a local hero, and certainly the most famous fighter from the Mississippi Coast. His coach was my coach, so I basically got a free gym membership. Cool, huh?

I rolled Camino through the plaza, passed a few strip

mall businesses and stopped right in front of the gym. Got out and locked up, thumbing the alarm fob. A trio of teenaged amateur boxers were walking out of the gym and stopped to ogle me, rap music bass notes loud then muted as the door closed behind them. The bright daylight showed their soaking wet shirts and loose pants clinging to them from hours of hard work. I could tell they had performed well because their little testosterone pumps were doing all the driving. All swagger and cockiness, chests poked out. One idiot blew a kiss at me. Another recognized me and punched the kiss blower in the arm, called him a choice expletive.

Every girl has a Shield of one form or another. Macho Shield, He's-Lying-To-Me-Shield. Whatever. Defense to cool down a man's B.S. Mine went up as a reaction to their idiocy, and, for whatever reason, I found myself cooing at them like they were the most adorable babies I have ever seen. "Aww ... Look at you little, wittle cutie pies! You are sooo handsome! Yes you are! Be careful going home to your mommies, now. Don't keep them worrying after the street lights come on."

Well now. Talk about an effective defuse. A woman's tears have a bio-chemical that short-circuits a man's libido. Talk to them the way I just did and they'll be lucky to have libidos for future encounters with females. The effect was more physical than expected, and I could almost see their man parts receding to safety somewhere in their stomachs, running away with cartoon feet. Leave me alone! I don't want to play anymore.

I am so immature today. What will I do when that's Nolan and his friends?

Damn. I know what I'll do. I'll be old.

I almost apologized to the boys, but two of them booked it into the parking lot, one so mad he could barely walk. The remaining kid stood there watching me, confused, face glowing.

The gym's door opened with a whoosh of musty warm air and upbeat music. My coach, Eddy, stepped out and scowled at the scarlet kid. "What are you doing, boy? You've had enough of your butt beat today. That girl there will make you a new butt and beat it, too. Now run along before she does it and I tell everyone you got whooped by a hundred-and-eighteen pound woman." The kid figured out how to walk. Eddy's threats were never empty; all part of his motivational program.

"Hey, Coach!" I hugged his neck like I haven't seen him in a while, even though I've been here with him every day for our eight-week training camp.

"Hey, darlin'. How are you doing?" His baritone had so much presence it made a little person like me vibrate when I stood next to him. He does a boss Darth Vader impression.

"I'm fine."

"Hey! I asked how you're doing, not how you looked."

"Such a kidder! Whatever, man," I giggled.

The old guy was a charmer. He's about sixty, five-eleven and two-fifty. Most people think he's Italian because of his demeanor and affiliations, though he's a French-Cajun mix. Huge hands and forearms capable of crushing just about anything. He took great pleasure from testing young guys' handshakes with his Grip of Death. Hilarious to watch. His smile put deep crow's feet around his eyes and made his under bite stick out like an English bulldog. A very macho bulldog. The chin beard and mustache were thick, cropped short and showed only a few gray hairs, belying his age. He let his hair grow out up top, dark and curly. The red, white and blue team jacket stretched almost comically across his huge chest and back was a remnant from his job coaching the U.S.A. Boxing Team many years ago. He could stand to lose a few pounds, maybe fit in his fave jacket again.

I sniffed it. "Have you been eating fried food?" I

inquired, frowning at him disapprovingly.

"No. Come on! Get off my case, girl. What did you say to those boys out there, anyway? They looked like hyenas running from a lion," he observed, changing the subject.

I let him get away with it. For now. "I know. Poor things. It's your fault. I hang out with you and Silvio too much. Rude-ass old men. I was mean to those boys. I felt terrible." I had unconsciously made a pouty face, sad eyes, heavy frown. I realized that's what Eddy was grinning at and shook off the emotion.

"You need to work on your sincerity," he said.

"Yeah, right! I do feel bad. Shut up."

He chuckled for a moment, then looked at his watch, his entire disposition subtly changing. Shifting. Like an inner toggle switch was clicked over to the Coach Function. "Let's take care of business. Get the wraps," he commanded.

"Yes, Coach," I answered, also switching mental gears. Eddy wasn't my friend while we trained. He was a butcher. And I was a masochist. We played out our roles to the fullest, and even won an award for it: the WBC bantamweight world championship belt. A thick green belt with pictures of former female champs on its wide band that flanked a huge golden WBC emblem. In two days, we'll put it on the line for a chance to unify titles with the WIBF. The World Boxing Council and Women's International Boxing Federation weren't happy that I planned to unify their titles then vacate them for retirement, but I wasn't worried about hurting their feelings too much, considering how much cheese they've made off me. The promoters and sanctioning bodies all worked together and against each other, a frustrating but fortune-making paradox that defined the economics of the Sweet Science.

Consuela Torres was the WIBF champ, and my current enemy. I planned to make her Shocker Victim #32. I wanted her belt.

I just realized for the first time that she probably wanted mine just as badly. Self-centered bitch.

Her, not me.

"Shocker! Wraps! Now."

"Yes, Coach."

I'll have to grill him on the health thing later. Scary to think the old guy could suffer a stroke, or worse, any minute. His food addiction is out of control, and I'm apparently the only one concerned about it.

But on the other hand, I don't want him to slim down too much. In my experience, fat coaches are the best of the best. Not sure why that is exactly, but there's proof to the statement. For example, look what keg belly Roy Jones did with his son, Roy, Jr. Or Michelin Man Lou Duva. How many world champions has he trained? Look on the sidelines of NFL games and you'll see the winning coaches have certainly partaken of their share of buffets. Andy Reid or Rex Ryan. All the fat boy high school and college coaches that inspire athletes to dominate. They kick butt and make the best motivators. Eddy is the same way, one of the best pugilist trainers in the country.

Yeah. Give me a fat coach over a fit coach any day. I walked past the gym's lone ring and got a good whiff of hot sweat. Two light heavyweight prospects, one black, the other white, were finishing up an intense session, slinging sweat all over the place. I loved it. The smell, the feeling of expended energy, the sounds of gloves and grunts and explosive exhalations.

Moving.

I don't mean moving in the way that Camino fires me up, semi-sexually. It's more literal: my motor controls, mind-muscle connection. I saw and heard these guys fighting – felt it – and instantly became a supercomputer that analyzed their moves to determine how I could counter them, destroy their rhythm and strategy. Made my heart thump slow and hard, made my vision and thoughts clearer, my skin more sensitive. My veins stood up like a threatened cat arches its back, hissing, coiled, ready for blistering speed and highly coordinated reflex.

Ronald smiled at me knowingly as I walked past. He leaned against a corner post pad, one hand holding a stopwatch above the black and white Title logo, the other arm draped over the top rope. He wore blue and white plaid shorts and a collared white short-sleeve deal that would look at home on the golf course. The red, white, and blue ropes shimmer-vibrated as his apprentices' sparring bounced them around the ring's white mat.

I stopped at a double-end bag mounting stand, a black post that was anchored to the floor several feet from the wall. The drop ceiling tiles and fluorescent lights were immaculate, lighting up a design that ran horizontally down the center of the wall around the gym. A pulsing design of a straight black line with intermittent triangles jutting out.

Vital signs. Punchline. With white highlights.

The line separated a two-tone job with gray below the line, a maroonish color up top, oddly similar to my truck's scheme. The colors meshed perfectly with the expulsions of breath, thuds of flesh being hit, the hip-hop bass, giving off an overall pleasant energy.

A gym bag hung from the steel post in front of me, cylindrical, two-feet long, made of a canvas that allowed air in and out. It was actually a tool bag, black with a red Craftsman tools logo, containing my hand wraps, jump rope, mouthpiece. I opened it and found socks and panties that stank of yesterday's sweat.

Eww. I hope no one looked in here...

I glanced around to see if anyone was smirking at me. Dis-fucking-gusting. I swear, my mom would disown me for such a violation of etiquette.

I peeked in a side pocket and found a few tampons and

my jock strap. Yeah, I use a jock. Women get hit there, too, and I promise you – it hurts. Let some cornbread fed hussy smoke you in the crotch with her manly arm. Balls or hoo-hah, it'll be unpleasant. But there was no sparring today, so I didn't need it.

I grabbed the wraps and hurried over to Eddy, who sat in a chair with a heat pack in one hand and held the back of another chair. My parking place. He scowled at me. I sat in the chair backwards, facing him, and scowled back. Though for a different reason, I'm sure. The sweat from the run was dried in my shorts and bra and made me feel gross. I guess I'm weird because I think dried sweat is yucky but didn't mind it fresh. The hot, wet musty stuff gives me a feeling like I'm a monster. A sweaty-ass beast. It's empowering. Like power posing, the physical affects the mental. Assume a confident posture, hands on hips, legs held apart and head held high with a serious mug. Look confident and you will be more confident. Put a puddle of sweat down your butt crack and under your boobs, some welts on your face and hands. Look like a monster. Feel like a monster. Be the goddamn thing.

Rock that monster, baby.

Eddy crushed the heat pack in his enormous paw, set it on my right shoulder to loosen the muscles there. Heat expansion to get things circulating and more flexible to avoid injury. Years of grueling exercise has taken its toll on my body, especially my shoulder. Every time it started aching I imagined the muscles in there forming fibrous faces and hands so they could scowl and flip me the bird.

Fuck you, lady! they say. We're not a slave cylinder!

I propped my hands over the back of the chair and he made quick work of wrapping them. The Ringside Products labels sewn onto the red material were showing on the wrists when he ended, signifying they were wrapped properly. He could do it blindfolded. With one hand.

He stood and adjusted the dark blue polo shirt over his stomach. The loose white shorts and Nikes he wore were practically his uniform. He settled the Team jacket over the back of a chair. "All right, girl. Get your butt in that ring and shadowbox. I want to see more head movement and pivots. Torres is going to come straightforward. Keep that in mind," he growled at me.

"Yes, Coach!"

He said, Jump. I said, How high? There is no questioning your trainer. You must trust them completely.

If there is any doubt, you will doubt yourself and lose your fights. It's that simple.

I got my butt in the ring eagerly. I trusted the belligerent old dude.

Explosive from the very first punch, I stretched out my left arm in a series of jabs, forcing my invisible opponent back into a corner, left foot tapping the mat in time with my jabs. I snapped off a right to the body, dipping and bending my knees quickly and blowing out a burst of air on the end of the punch.

Focus on exhaling, not the inhale. Relax muscles, control breathing. Takes about ten minutes before I can get into a rhythm. Have to get through the first wind and hitch a ride on the second.

I shifted my weight from foot-to-foot, weaving my head under and to the sides, slipping phantom punches. Fast, light, delicate. Flowing. Then I countered, pivoting to the right and launching my money punch straight right into my Shadow's chin.

BAM!

I backpedaled until my back hit the ropes, blocked an uppercut, countered with a left-hook, being sure to step into it and really twist my hips and shoulders. Have to get this baby torquing properly if we want to preserve my right shoulder and use the hook for a knockout.

"More of that! I want a hundred hooks! You're too square. Point that shoulder!" Coach yelled. His eyes were constantly moving, tracking the invisible opponent and my interaction with her. He didn't miss a thing.

I danced around to get more relaxed, threw some combos. Uh-oh. Getting warmed up now. Look out phantom! I'm kinda fast. I juked, ducked, jived, zigged, weaved, zagged. Set up my opponent with a snapping right, then dropped my left arm to make them come forward and try to land something in the opening. A trap that almost always works because it's instinctual for a boxer to go for it. I imagined Torres coming forward with her one-two and I dropped back on my right heel to avoid it while stepping toward her with my left foot and throwing a hard, punishing hook over the top of her arm, into her jaw.

Gotcha.

"Get over here!" Eddy hollered, all hyped up, climbing into the ring with some punch mitts and a pair of ten-ounce gloves. The mitts were black and red, Title brand, tiny looking on the end of his big arms. The gloves were pink. I like pink everything. It's perhaps the only feminine affinity in my world of manly activities. They were the only pair in the joint that color. Ronald got them for me so I wouldn't have to share sweaty gear with the men. What a gentleman, right? Not that I really minded sharing, but he insisted on it because some guys get off on women's sweaty things. I pointed out that that goes both ways.

He replied, "Yeah. But if a guy caught you sniffing their sweat, they'd love it. Whereas, if you caught a guy huffing your fumes, you'd get weirded out or try to hurt them."

The man had a point. It could be troublesome.

My gloves streaked toward Eddy's mitts like pink tracers, feminine missiles with bad intentions. Punches popping on the pads like bottle rockets zipping through the air and voicing their report at the end.

Pop-pop!

I jabbed and threw a right. He threw a right-hand mitt at me, faster than belief. Gunfighter fast. I ducked, weaved under and toward him a half-second before tagging a hook into his other mitt.

BAM!

It echoed around the room, hardest hook you can throw. Load it up with that much leverage and weight distribution on the inside of your opponent's guard and you might break their neck.

We practiced it over and over, programming my muscle-memory. I imagined Torres being wary of my notoriously dangerous right-hand, watching for an opening, thinking she'll willingly take one of my "weak" lefts in order to land her power punches. Instead of countering with my right as she expects, I'll weave and hook.

Drop the bitch.

Did I tell you we practiced it over and over?

We quit after my arms turned into noodles. I grabbed my jump rope, red and pink plastic beads, and found a spot on the floor no one was using. There were a lot more people coming into the gym now. Some older guys, most young. One girl. All mix of races, some very puzzling mixes.

Eddy watched me. I watched Ronald. He was getting a little frustrated showing a step-and-punch drill to a very uncoordinated white dude. Really talented boxers like Ronald usually don't make great trainers. Good, maybe, but not great. They have trouble understanding why other people can't do what they do, and lose patience. I told him he'd be a better trainer if he gained fifty pounds. It came out sounding like a joke, but I was serious. Take away his physical ability and he'd get a different perspective on things, understand why others couldn't move like he did.

Hip-hop music thundered a nice rise and fall in the flow of sound. Lil Wayne, beating up the speakers. I jumped my beaded rope in front of a wall of mirrors, dancing out a heel-toe tap in a pattern that few can do. Quick and powerful. Precise and delicate. A ballerina riding a Harley popped in my head and I burst into a fit of giggles that slowed me down.

"Earth to Shocker! I don't know what you're thinking, but if you can't focus, I'll put on some country music. Pick it up a step!" Eddy threatened, glaring at the guys that overheard and laughed.

I wiped the smile off and started lots of double jumps and sprints. Mixed it with dancing all over the damn place. Rocking my monster. The threat of sad, slow, very unmotivating country music always gets me focused and willing to do extra effort. Eddy knew how to focus fighters with the precision of a microscope; all part of his motivational program.

I was drenched in sweat, but my heart pounded out a calm, hard drumming and was nowhere near being taxed. My breathing quickened as I kept up the faster pace, but remained even and controlled. I was really clowning now, doing a modified tango with my lovely, colorful beaded partner.

Intergalactic by the Beastie Boys started thumping and my feet matched the rhythm at a double-pace. Eddy and another trainer were watching my feet with critical eyes. The younger guys were watching my butt in the mirror. I dropped down to do some frog jumps and some hick started yipping like a dog, a cheer like this was a country hoedown and I was center stage, showing up the competition.

"Time! Sprint!" Eddie yelled.

I stood and knocked out a two-minute sprint finale, running in place and spinning the hell out of the rope. My breathing became labored, sweat gushed and flew off my arms and legs, yet none of that was my focus. I couldn't help but watch the redneck cheerleader. He was clapping,

35

stomping, and smiling like a crazy man at a Merle Haggard concert. All he needed was a moonshine jug and a spit cup.

Will somebody tell this fool yipping and clapping to the Beastie Boys was a capital offense? He looked retarded, for Christ's sake.

"Time! No break! Give me the rope and shadowbox!" Eddie said, grabbing the rope in mid-spin, pointing at the mirrors.

I didn't waste breath with a response. I turned and beat the crap out of my reflection. Throwing one blistering combination after another, completely focused on my body and thoughts of strategy to outbox an opponent that could match me punch for punch. Impossible to beat your reflection. A motherfucker of a challenge to try.

To really try.

I ignored the background in the reflection. Guys standing around with arms crossed, hands on waists, smiling at the sweat showing on the crack of my shorts or overawed at this bantamweight chick that could kick their ass in the ring any day of the week.

"Time!" Eddy stormed up to me, rattled off a dozen things I was doing wrong. Needed to drop my butt more on pivots, keep weight in the middle of my stance. I was too square, showing too much torso to my opponent. Needed to tuck my chin more on the jab. Everybody else was exclaiming how perfect I looked, how great my form was. Bunch of Yes Men. Eddy was the only one that told me I needed to improve, keeping me from becoming over-confident while driving me like a mule.

Cue snapping whip sound. Yah, mule! Yah! Butcher and masochist. I love my fat ass coach!

"No sparring today," Eddy said. "You have peaked. Sleep good tonight and after the weigh-in tomorrow we'll get you rehydrated and do some light cardio." He gave me a serious look. "The fight is in two days. Are you ready?"

"I'm gonna Shocker."

"Believe it."

He handed me a towel and placed an ice pack on my shoulder, signaling the end of our workout. We sat in our chairs in comfortable silence as I toweled my face and neck and he unwrapped my hands. We stood, he handed me the wraps. Hugged me. I left a big sweaty stain on one half of his body.

Cool.

He lumbered off toward some guys sparring in the ring, calling out their mistakes, driving them harshly to perform better.

I absolutely ached for a drink of water. So much that I felt my throat tighten with a feeling that wasn't dryness. My eyes watered. Or tried to. Some cute teenaged dude approached with a bottle of Evian he had bought just for me, blushing. Aw shucks, ma'am. Sweet. I thanked him, took the bottle, turned my back to him and glared at the bottle, the water that I couldn't drink but wanted more than I ever wanted anything in my life. A primitive instinct for survival deep in the lizard brain genes I carried screamed at me to gnaw off the cap and suck the liquid life out of the container.

Drink it! Drink it, you crazy bitch! Do you want to die?! it said. It screamed. It demanded.

I would have cried if I could have made tears.

I opened it. Poured a splash in my desert mouth. Moaned like a porn star skank, and started choking when I realized my loud cry of pleasure was heard by one of the trainers and his apprentice. They nodded and smiled at me. I grinned sheepishly, held up the bottle like it was the water's fault.

The front door opened and my husband and son walked in. I wasn't surprised to see my man, Alan. He routinely visited to watch my training and hang out with Ronald or Eddy. But my stepson Nolan had made it clear that he didn't like me in this place, didn't approve of his supposed-to-be mom in here or in the ring fighting. To his eight-year-old mind, that is Not Right.

I think for that reason he still has not called me Mom or Mother. He calls me Clarice, and I'm okay with that. I understand that gaining his love and showing him he has gained mine is a long-term process. A frustrating, glacier slow process of wanting to scream and curse and cry, spit, smack, throw, stomp, pull hair and scream some more.

And I'm okay with that. Damn, I need some water.

They walked up and I smiled at Nolan. "Hey, my man. You're looking sharp in those new shoes," I said.

He looked down at his new boots, shrugged. The Timberlands made him look like a little gentleman, and that's how I tried to talk to him. He couldn't stand it when people talked to him like a child. He looked up at me, cute, slim face showing he was going to be a tall, lanky dude with an angular jaw. Just like his dad. He had a shaggy haircut that was annoyingly in style these days, dark brown and curled just a hint on the tips. Blue eyes, a dozen freckles over his nose and cheeks, also just like his dad. A blue and green t-shirt with an Alien Workshop skateboard logo matched the Silver Tab jeans and brown leather boots perfectly

"Yeah, they're okay," he finally responded, looking at my soaking wet clothes with an odd, almost disgusted expression. Broke my heart. I didn't know what to do to change it. I was thinking fast when Ronald showed up and saved me.

"Hey, Nolan!" Ronald greeted, his wonderful smile flashing. His face and presence and energy made the guy off-the-charts personable. Nolan really liked him, and his face lit up to show it.

"What's going on, Ronald?" Nolan piped in his adorably high-pitched voice. I once told him he sounded manly, but he didn't go for it. Turned into another strike out for Team Mom.

They grabbed hands, one cool guy to another. Ronald asked him, "You reading that Bible I gave you? How are those grades looking?" He didn't bend down towards Nolan like an adult addressing a child. He stood up straight, talking to him like he would anyone else. Ronald was great with kids in that way. The youngsters running around the gym felt safe here. Felt that comfort that's necessary to have to build confidence. Kids excelled here because the trainers knew how to instill self-esteem, inspiring them to listen to the discipline and dream and take steps to achieve those dreams, which perpetuates more confidence. Some of these guys needed a wheelbarrow to tote their balls when they left.

Nolan responded to the place just like the other kids. He just had it in his head that mothers weren't supposed to be fighters. Not Right.

What could I do? Retire.

That's why this was going to be my last fight. I wanted to develop my family.

Ronald led Nolan away for some man talk, and I looked over at my husband. He stared into my eyes, standing there with his hands in his pockets, smiling a half-smile that made one eye squint a little. An expression that tells the room this guy Knows Stuff.

Quiet genius look. Smoking, freaking hot. I loved this man.

"Hello, Ace," I murmured, wiping a finger along my forehead. Flicked sweat at him.

He wiped it from his face, half-smile turning into a grin. "Dear," he acknowledged. His blue eyes were ridiculously clear, burning with intelligence and sneaky thoughts. He looked like an older Nolan, but with less freckles and his hair was dyed blonde, a spikey surfer's cut. He's tall, six-three, one-seventy. Lanky and wiry. A little timid at times, but I like that introvert geek thing. His Guess short sleeve button-up matched the dark yellow Billabong shorts and leather moccasins.

"Nice kicks, husband. You buy me anything?" I asked, smiling. "I see you found some shorts long enough to cover those coconut knees."

"Hey! Don't get me started on your knees, and what you do on them." I tried to shush him, but it was in vain; the trainer and boxer working out next to us got another earful of eroticism at my expense and I blushed furiously. Ace grinned and continued. "And, anyway. 'You buy me anything?' is no way to ask about my health and spirits this morning."

I harrumphed. "You look like a damn beach ad and have that smirk of delight on your mug. You're doing great. So. Did. You. Buy. Me. Anything?" I said, poking him in the chest, pushed him.

He pushed me back – with a delicious smack on the lips. "Nope."

"Fucker."

"Okay, I did. But you can't have it because you were mean," he teased.

"Then I apologize, Alan, my Ace. So how was your morning?" I tried again.

But he didn't go for it. "Nope." He smiled real big and turned to walk around me.

I followed. "But I apologized."

"You need to work on your sincerity."

"No, I don't! I am sorry. Why does everybody keep saying that? Shut up."

He walked over to the chairs Eddy and I used, sat in one, crossing an ankle over his knee. He looked over at Nolan and waved when Nolan looked up from running on a treadmill. Our son was laughing, telling Ronald to make it go faster. Seeing that boy laugh should have made me feel happy, but it didn't quite take me there. I wanted to feel it. But because I wasn't able to make him laugh, I couldn't share the joy. The only thing I felt at the moment was an irrational jealousy of Ronald.

Stupid emotions.

"What's the matter?" Ace said, sensing my mood change. He looked at Nolan and Ronald. Back to me. "I told him after this fight you were going to be at home with us more. Doing mommy stuff."

"Thanks. That's sweet, Ace. I'll talk to him before I leave tonight. I know it's been really hard for him. For all of us. I want to share so much with him, but he just pushes me away. Says I'm not his mother."

Ace stood and put his arms around my shoulders, quietly offering his support. My head rested below his chest, a warm, tall pillar of unconditional love. He knew I'm always emotional before a fight because my body is so out of whack. And after the fight. And at a certain time of the month.

And sometimes for no reason at all. Little ol' emotional me. I blame Camino.

I patted his chest, gave him a quick and grateful smile. "I'm good, man. Let's get out of here and have a little Us-Time before I have to head for the airport." I grabbed the back of his neck, pulled his head down and whispered in his ear, "I've been horny all morning. Thinking about you, big guy."

He got a really silly grin that widened as his ears reddened. What a beautiful sight.

Did I do that?

He said, "So Camino shakes up the bottle and I get to pop the cork, huh?"

"Oh, that's not...man! You know I –"

"Mmm-hmm. I can't wait. The caress of your sweaty body at the end of the day is the only thing that keeps me going." He stroked a finger down my cheek. "Sexy. I just have to have it."

The trainer and apprentice snickered next to us. I glared at them, mind your business, please. Looked back at Ace, shaking a fist under his nose. "You are gonna get it, fucker. And I'm gonna be the one to –"

"Give it to you," he finished. Then he sniffed me and made a Stinky Face. "Can't wait." His voice oozed sarcasm. But smooth and sexy sarcasm. His grin made his eyes disappear.

I hooked him in the ribs and laughed at his grunt. The Nosy Nelsons laughed, too. I walked over to Eddy while Ace told Nolan we were leaving. Coach was doing his thing with the mitts, working with a young white dude. "Hey, Coach! I'm leaving. See you at the airport."

"All right, darlin'. You already know the drill. No shower. Don't soak up any water or drink it, either. Have Ace work some acupressure on that shoulder and help with deep stretches. Don't forget," he instructed, a variation of a lecture I've heard dozens of times. He told me all this without taking his eyes from his task. He circled the guy, catching punches, ring creaking under his weight.

"Gotcha, Coach. Later!"

Ronald walked with my guys to the door where I waited. He stuck his fist out to me and I bumped mine into his, one boxer to another. "Don't hurt Torres too bad," he said, winking.

I winked back. "It's said that I'm insane in the ring. Therefore, I can't be held liable for my actions. Torres is screwed."

"Bring home another belt. See you later, Nolan. Ace." He held the door for us and mussed Nolan's shag as we walked out.

The smell of exhaust was heavy on the breeze as people motored away from nearby businesses to their lunch breaks.

The sun on Nolan's dark hair showed streaks of red in the back and a dash of black on the sides, making me curious about his bio-mother and where she came from. Alan, or Ace, as everybody called him, didn't talk about her, preferring to keep the past in the past.

It was hard to argue a constructive concept such as that, so I remained quiet on the subject. And curious, dammit.

The silver Dodge Ram SRT-10 was parked next to my El Camino. An awe-inspiring sight. The paint glittered with subtle metallic flakes, almost like an early morning dew was permanently clinging to it. The hood scoop fed air to the 500HP Viper V10 engine, and the wide, lowered stance with custom racing wheels, aerodynamic body panels and bed cover made it the fastest production truck built to date.

Ace's baby. Well, one of them.

The mind-boggling array of electronics in the dash, the wires running to the various computer monitors and unidentifiable components on the floorboard and console, were a dead giveaway to the origin of my husband's nickname. He was an electronics wizard.

A former hacker that worked for Wikileaks, he was forced into retirement after being arrested for breaking into the Pentagon's Human Resources database. He didn't actually get caught – he was too good for that – but his Wikileaks bosses got busted with the data and sold him out to avoid spending time in federal prison. I asked him why he got himself involved in something like that.

"For fun," he said. Simple as that.

That burning, sneaky intelligence in his eyes? It constantly demanded that he challenge it. It challenged his sneaky butt with five years of probation, too.

Seeing the gizmos in his console always made me think of the day he brought this truck into my mechanic shop for servicing about two years ago. I saw the electronics setup he had built and nearly had an orgasm on his leather seats. Yet another instance where my involuntary cry of pleasure embarrassed me silly.

He liked my reaction to it, of course.

The language he used to explain his creations wasn't humanoid. At best, it could be called Geek Speak. I threatened to kick his ass if he ever did anything illegal again, then hired him to design a diagnostic machine. I needed one that interfaced with Internet automotive databases and software programs for any vehicle, for any purpose imaginable.

Hey, I'm an automotive wizard. No telling what I'll cook up in my shop.

Ace designed much more than that. We now have iPhone apps that can locate anything to do with the auto or engineering world. And apps that can run diagnostics on anything from a Scion to a Bentley.

I asked him why he did all this.

"For fun," he said with his smoking hot half-smile. I told him we were going to start dating, just snatched him up by his shirt and demanded that he take me to dinner.

"Yes, dear," he said for the first time. And I kissed him for the first time.

I knew for months that he liked me but was too shy to ask me out – why else would he show up for "work" every day when he wasn't yet an employee, and had finished what I had hired him for in the first week? That made his charm irresistible; I admire persistence. He seemed content with me being the assertive one of our relationship, and told me so. Since then our personalities have meshed like a ring and pinion, one turning the other, one unable to work without the other.

When he introduced me to Nolan, it jumpstarted my maternal and family instincts. Completely freaked me out, to be honest. Re-wired my biology and view of life. I suddenly wanted a family. Now I have one with a man I love.

We just needed a little fine-tuning, that's all.

After this fight I was going to be the mother Nolan needed and a better wife to Alan. No more traveling all over the world to fight, staying gone for months at a time for training camps in Europe or Mexico. No more distressing my son because his mommy is leaving him behind for a dangerous job in an unknown place.

A revelation occurred to me: I'll have to leave part of myself behind. Say *adios* to Shocker and her life of adrenaline and fame. The physical and mental challenge of training that I loved so much.

The vast crowds cheering my name...

Could I give all that up? Most boxers had trouble doing it.

I told myself I was gaining a lot more in doing so. Lord, I hope this worked out.

I looked at Nolan and smiled. He turned away from me, opened the passenger door on the Dodge and climbed in. Slammed it. Put his iPod headphones on.

I frowned at Ace.

He said, "I know, dear. He's been acting like that ever since I told him you were leaving to fight again."

"But it's only two days this time. That's why we did the training camp here. It's over after this." He shrugged, not knowing what to do either. "Damn. I'll talk to him."

I climbed into the driver's seat and shut the door, leather and the unique scent of running computers filling my nose. I looked at the kid and felt the kind of nervousness that hits me just before a fight. I inhaled slowly, held it, let it out and gently cleared my throat.

He finally looked at me, paused his music. "What do you want?" he sulked. He turned the music on and off and I could hear Lady Gaga jamming from the headphones, the truck's silent cab amplifying it.

"Nolan, honey, I want to know what you want.

Whatever is on your mind, please just tell me, okay?"

He fidgeted with the headphone wire, twirling it around a finger. "I don't want you to fight anymore," he said with a pout, looking down at his lap.

I don't know where the water came from, but a tear burned the crap out of my eye. I tried to work a little spit in my mouth so I could answer, reining in the urge to cry. "I promise you this is the last time. Look at me, sweetheart." He looked at me sideways, mouth still turned down, pouting. The tear escaped and ran down my cheek. "I promise you. I'll be home in two days, and I'll never leave you and your daddy like this again. Next time I travel somewhere, I'm bringing my two handsome men with me. Okay, honey?" My voice broke. My dry throat locked up so tight I thought I was going to suffocate right in front of him.

Rein it in, lady. Relax.

Now, breathe.

Nolan watched me for a minute, his own eyes watery now. He looked back at his lap and sniffed a suddenly runny nose. "You promise?" he said.

"I promise," I croaked. Then patted his head, kissed his cheek. I had to get some air. I turned and jumped out, closed the door and managed to contain a scream of frustration.

Ace walked over to me. "You going to live?" he asked with concern, handing me a bottle of water.

I grabbed it, yanked off the top. Squirted. Swished. Spat. Moaned like I was dying. "Yeah. I think. God, this is not a good mental state before a fight."

"Well, I believe I have something that will cheer you up."

"You're going to get naked right here?"

"Um. No. Sorry, do you want me to?"

"Come on, dude. What do you have for me?"

"Since you aren't being a meany now, come check it out."

He walked around to the back of the truck and stuck a

key in the bed cover. Opened it. A huge alien rat costume was laid out on the bed in plastic bags. The mask, in its own bag, had big eyes with clear lenses that would glow multiple colors when the LEDs were switched on, long eyelashes, a Mohawk, and thick red lips. Wicked, but cute and girlish. "Ladies and gentlemen..." He did a drum roll on the tailgate. "Shocker's last show!" he announced with a wave and bow. That one squinted eye and half-smile appeared again.

Knows Stuff.

I started squirming.

"Aw. It's perfect," I said. Hugged him, kissed him. "You're right, Ace. This did cheer me up."

"A female boxing rat beast in a cage of lightning. Should be worthy of a Shocker show."

"No doubt, man. I'm gonna sing *Bullet With Butterfly Wings* on the way to the ring."

"So you're actually going to sing it, not just play the song?"

"It's a Smashing Pumpkins song. I can scream like Billy Corgan."

"Do it." He crossed his arms, raised his eyebrows.

"I don't have any spit. I'd sound worse than a rat beast right now. But I can sing." I poked him in the chest and gave him a look that dared him to dispute my boast.

"Yes, dear. I finished the LCDs and sent them to Silvio, built as you ordered. The cage setup is probably in Philadelphia by now."

"You brilliant man. You are too good to me. Let's go home so I can spank you properly."

"Spank?"

"I said thank you."

"Yes, dear."

PART III

TWELVE MILES from the Philadelphia Airport my destiny awaited. The cornerstone that will cap the legacy of Shocker the Fighter and initiate a new era for Clarice the Woman. The Wife and Mother.

North Broad Street was filled with old buildings, but none was more distinguished than the four-story beauty that was the Blue Horizon. The legendary boxing venue was over a hundred and forty years old. It pulsed with an ancient force beyond its years, a residual energy that permeated the structure's core from the hundreds of thousands of fans that have screamed within these walls. I could feel that energy now, revitalized from the crowd of fifteen hundred that surrounded the ring and voiced their joy from the previous fight, a ten-rounder between welterweight contenders. If I read the commotion correctly, someone got knocked the fuck out.

Woo-hoo! Always an inspiring sound.

The exterior and design of the Blue Horizon were exquisite, but the interior showed the aged and worn characteristics of an establishment with a maintenance budget deficit. Well loved, well used. Reminded me of Camino's 1959 patinaed paint and body. It had needed to be restored but broke my heart to do so because I was reluctant to change his O.G. personality, rough and gruff. This joint had that O.G. effect. Rough, dirty, powerful, like it was the Grandpa of Philly. A mean old son of a bitch of a grandpa that would outlive God, kick His ass every time it thundered, and turn His angels into his own personal harem with a schlong as big as a mountain.

Old School architectural pimp. Hell yeah.

The locker room floor tiles were white, chipped and pitted with black mold stains, and sprouted benches along the walls and down the center of the small, rectangular room. The walls were thick concrete with peeling white paint and brown stains from strong disinfectant that didn't like to wipe off. Fluorescent lights with dirty globes shined dimly over our heads. It smelled like it looked, old and dank, with detergents that couldn't quite mask the odor of degeneration.

Like my grandpa.

The walls vibrated with the crowd's energy, towering resonators that shook my little bones with immeasurable power and buzzed my head with sensations that mirrored my thoughts and intentions for the upcoming battle.

Hyper thoughts. Violent intentions.

My mouth was suddenly dry, my bladder full. Symptoms a soldier experiences before going into a deadly war she knows she may not make it out of in one piece. That feeling of High Risk that takes the mind into an alternate reality where instincts do all the driving and leave all the drama and whiny emotions in the dust. A nervous want. A fear of blood loss and a desire for blood lust.

A Sweet Science.

The strategy of Hurt and Not Get Hurt. The strategy of You Better Fucking Win Because There Is No Second Place.

I wanted it.

My monster wanted it, the fight junkie dwelling in my head.

"I want it," I told Eddy. He straddled the bench in front of me, wrapping my hands, ignoring the Philadelphia Boxing Commission representative and the Latino dude from Team Torres that looked over his shoulder to monitor his work.

"Believe it, girl. You'll get it. She's all yours," he said, adjusting the sleeve of his black and pink Team Ares jacket, unrolled another length of tape. The white athletic tape he layered on my fists tightened, hardened my hands into lethal weapons. Grenades I planned to decimate Torres' head and body with. I tensed, my foot started bouncing. Eddy started taping faster, his mind on the same alternate realm as mine.

I wanted it. He wanted it.

Now.

"Tell them to just play the song. I can't sing it. Don't know what the hell I was thinking," I told him.

He looked over at my promoter, Silvio, who sat on a bench to our left, brushing imaginary dust off his black Hugo Boss suit. Smiled at him. Looked back at me, underbite sticking out with a grin. "I already took care of it," he said.

I scowled at him. "Really," I responded, adding a glare to my mugging.

"Don't worry, darlin'. No one doubts your singing ability. Your ability to overcome the killer instinct you feel now, and perform a song you've only practiced in your car. That was in doubt."

"Really."

"And like you just said, what were you thinking? This isn't a singing contest. Forget about it."

"Yeah, Shock. Forget about it," Silvio said, adding his two cents and earning a glare-scowl from me. The Commission rep snickered and I aimed my mean mug at him. He quickly gained his composure.

"Let's get these gloves on. Then you get your butt in that contraption. It's show time," Eddy said.

"Yes, Coach," I growled at him. He just continued his stupid grin and unwound the final length of tape. Cut it, stuffed the roll in a jacket pocket. Taped my hand.

Silvio had several event assistants running around double-checking his commands. The referee walked in, a late-fifties white dude with a smooth, tan, cosmetically enhanced face and Just For Men gelled brown hair. A herd of people and cameras followed, HBO Pay-Per-View staff. The commission rep signed his mark on my hand wraps and I stuffed them into the gloves Eddy held. Eight-ounce Cleto Reyes, black. He taped the wrists of the gloves quickly, securing the laces. The commission guy scribbled his mark over the tape, a seal that proved the gloves weren't loaded and prevented tampering between here and the ring. The ref stepped forward and did his thing, instructing me to avoid illegal punches and obey his commands at all times. The cameras zoomed in on us. I agreed to obey. He turned and walked through the HBO staff, who directed cameras after me as I walked into the hallway.

The "contraption" sat outside the locker room door, in the hall that led into the Carmichael Auditorium where the crowd and ring awaited. Event assistants swarmed me. The huge rat costume was thrown over my shoulders, around my pink and black trunks and legs. Zipped up. The head was placed over mine so that my eyes, nose, and mouth popped out under the rat's snout. The clear plastic spikes that ran over the rat's crown and down the spine were turned on, LEDs flickering white and purple. The feminine mask and wild, mutated dark brown furry body made me feel like Godzilla's bitch.

Hell yeah. I could dig it.

I noticed the microphone had been removed from the snout and figured Eddy had done it before I even arrived. Old bastard, doubting my singing skills. I ought to take him to the fried seafood buffet and order us salads. Watch him sweat like a druggie in a crack house that's only allowed to smoke cigarettes. Teach the ol' geezer...

Music started, interrupting my thoughts of revenge. *She Wolf* by Shakira blasted from the auditorium, pummeling the walls and pillars with the Latin superstar's lilting voice and dance beats. The crowd roared its delight and I could picture women of all ages shaking their hips and waving their arms over their heads. Standard protocol for a Shakira jam.

Silvio appeared beside me, waving the cameras back. "Shocker, baby. You look fierce! Phenomenal!" he yelled over the resonations. The hallway was like a huge bass port, the air moving with the sound waves and fluttering all around us. Silvio's cologne wafted in my face. Polo Black with a dash of Cuba's finest tobacco.

"You're wearing too much cologne," I told him.

"What?"

"I'll miss this when I get home!"

"I will, too. You're the best, doll!" he yelled back.

I hugged him, decided against informing him that no amount of Polo could hide a Havana Sweet; he'd never fool his nagging wife. Stepped into my cage. Assistants stepped forward and secured the Plexiglas door. A toggle switch was positioned next to the doorframe. I flipped it. The clear liquid crystal displays on the outside of the Plexiglas walls, roof, and floor burst with bright blue, white, and purple streaks of lightning. It was so realistic looking it made you believe you could hear it sizzle and pop, anticipating thunderclaps. I smiled, thinking of Ace and the mad scientist laugh he must have guffawed after creating this thing.

Shakira quit shaking the fans' rumps, returning to dormant 0s and 1s in a digital hard drive somewhere in a tiny control room out of sight. The crowd calmed to a simmer. The ring announcer boomed his intro for Consuela Torres, giving her kudos for being the WIBF champ with a record of twenty-six wins, zero losses, and eight knockouts.

A nice account with ample embellishment.

The sound system started wailing again, this time with the heavy guitar chords of Smashing Pumpkins. Billy Corgan, *Bullet with Butterfly Wings*. My gloves and boots started moving of their own volition, anticipating the show they had trained so hard for, bouncing on my toes, shuffling my fists. Four huge bodybuilders in white lab coats walked into the hall, scientists to carry their experimental rat beast in a cage. They took up positions at the four corners, grabbed the handles and lifted the eight-by-six box of lightning above their shoulders, started walking slowly towards the auditorium.

I am the Shocker. Thirty-one fights and twenty-nine knockouts. A feat that hasn't been matched in my weight class, or in any of the classes below a hundred-and-sixty-eight pounds. I looked at my right arm. All of the KOs owed credit to it. It's a lot bigger than my left. Not as fast, but a hell of a lot more powerful. A sixteen-year mechanic's arm, formed since I began turning wrenches at ten, that made me pound-for-pound the hardest hitting gal in boxing history. I wanted to use The Mechanic as my fight name, but inadvertently let Silvio see me shock myself one morning when he came into my shop.

Hey, I was out of coffee. Had a shitload of work to do.

He wouldn't let it go. Insanely original, and would pique the interest of the world, he said. The slick hustler was right. That stunt had landed us some pretty big paydays, for women's boxing, and landed me the name Shocker. A huge portion of the crowd was chanting it right now.

Goosebumps tingled up and down my arms, little icicles sprouting up under the beads of sweat.

Hyper thoughts. Violent intentions.

"Despite of my rage/ I am still just a rat in a cage!" Billy Corgan sang as we entered the auditorium proper, verse timed perfectly. I started shadowboxing, dancing, dipping, pivoting, boots squeaking on plastic, throwing combos with easy speed, a freak in an electrical storm. The crowd loved it. The scientists and their insane creation, a monster they intended to turn loose inside the ring.

I rocked my monster, feeling the crowd's pleasure fuel my drive and really get my motor running. I lived for this moment. Nothing else was ever important or ever would be. This was, is, and will be my life, my destiny, my legacy. My life was on the line, and I planned to shine.

It was Shocker's time to shine.

The music ended, the cage was lowered, the door was opened. I bounded out in a crouch, still shadowboxing. The crowd stood to see my costume and bellowed their approval. The monster was loose. Huge TV monitors above the ring showed Godzilla's bitch bounding toward the ring's steps in a frenzy of pumping gloves, snarls, whipping tail and lightning Mohawk, clowning and working her Monster Mash.

I don't remember climbing the steps or ducking under the ropes. Suddenly, I was in the ring, in a frenzy, in character and mashing my role to the fullest. I stopped on cue, as the music stopped, and Eddy lifted the mask off my head. Assistants unzipped the costume and it disappeared under the ropes. The TV monitors showed Eddy standing behind me, rubbing my right shoulder. I looked up at myself, looking at myself. Face a thunderhead, brows furrowed, eyes dark and ominous, mouth in a snarl, boobs strapped down under my black tank. I raised my left glove to salute the fans. They cheered and raised their arms in reply.

The ring announcer grabbed the microphone that was lowered from the overhead scaffolding. "Ladies and gentlemen! Introducing the reigning WBC world bantamweight champion!" he proclaimed smoothly, with super-sized garnishment to make it all sound pretty and important. I loved his voice. Who didn't? A brief pause to let the audience applaud, then he continued. "With a record of thirty-one wins, zero losses, and twenty-nine knockouts! The UNIQUE and PETITE! Clarice-'Shockerrr' – Areees!"

The cheers lit up my pleasure centers like they never have before, pumping me full of my favorite drug: Invincibility. The rooty-poot term "confident" didn't begin to describe my current mental state. The wonder drug the fans have immersed me in has inflated my ego to universal proportions, expanding like the Big Bang, flowing through my entire body and bonding to every molecule like armor. I'm bulletproof, baby. An invincible predator. And tonight I'm going to jail for murder.

Torres is going in the ground.

The referee called his combatants to the center of the ring. Put his latex-gloved hands on a shoulder of each of us and spoke into the microphone, reminding us of the instructions he gave us earlier in our locker rooms. I glared at my enemy. Looked her up and down. Growled because her light blue trunks with gray fur looked way cuter than mine. Her gray tank, no boobs, and manly shoulders didn't match her very feminine heart-shaped face and button nose. Big eyes and thick lips, dark hair in micro-braids, tied in a ponytail. Prominent Latin features. She looked down at the mat, a psychological tactic that worked as a confidence tool for most fighters. I had invincible overconfidence shooting out of me like lunch from a supermodel, so glaring was the only function I had at that point.

The ref wrapped it up, the microphone was reeled up. The trainers and Teams ducked out of the ring. We went to our corners.

Ding! Round One.

The blue mat didn't sound a peep as our bantam-weighted boots circled the Tecate beer logo in the center of the twenty-foot square ring. We circled to our left, two right-handed boxers dipping knees, weaving heads.

Feigning jabs. Torres lunged forward with a double-jab and I pivoted to my right while countering with a quick right-hand punch. Missed. She avoided it with ease, obviously having trained for that move. We circled some more. I stopped, flat-footed for a ruse. Torres lunged again, a viper striking with liquid grace. Shifting my weight to my right foot, I threw a jab that slid right down her arm and, BAM! Solidly thumped her button nose.

Damn, that felt good. First landed punch is always the best. Like an alcoholic taking her first sip of the day. Ah! Give me more.

It is on, you little bull. Toro, bitch! TORO!

Torres' corner started yelling to her in Spanish. She attacked, jabbing, trying to sneak in an uppercut to the body. I jabbed to fend her off, pivoted to my left, back to the right, catching her punches on my gloves, waiting on her to fire another right-hand. There it comes! My focus was so acute everything slowed down like a scene in The Matrix, surreal, megamo. As her punch reached the end of its range, I ducked under it, weaved out over my left foot, shot a left-hook towards her ear like a Tomahawk missile, really thrusting up from legs and transferring that weight and momentum into my twisting shoulders and through the punch.

Through her head.

BOOM!

Sweat exploded off her head, spraying the panel of judges that sat ringside behind a table. One of the judges, an elderly lady with snow-white hair, wiped her face and grinned.

Torres wobbled into the ropes and I attacked with four and five punch combinations that had the crowd on their feet, screaming with glee. The Invincible dope and bloodlust overcame me and I stupidly wasted more energy than I should have.

Torres was hurt but still firing back, still defending. As it turned into a slugfest, the cheers became deafening, teasing, taunting and enticing me with more of the Good Stuff, urging me to keep throwing. Keep chasing that first-hit reward. Torres felt it, too, and was beginning to land more punches as my shoulders tired.

Eddy yelled and my senses returned, telling me to get out of there, let go of the bloodlust, put a leash on the fight junkie. "Box! Box!" Eddy shouted. "Move your butt, girl!"

I needed to get her back on my terms, control the fight with boxing instead of punching. Slugging is what Torres did best. I needed to pick her apart like a surgeon. I jabbed out, away from her, moving back to the center of the ring for more movement options. She followed, gliding smoothly and showing no signs that she had been hurt.

Did I hurt her? Or did that bitch trick me into punching it out with her?

"Ugh!" I grunted in frustration.

Torres jabbed, threw a right that I blocked. She did it again, but feigned the right. Too late, I fell for it, threw a counter-right that missed and gave her the opening she had set me up for. She snapped her hips and whopped me in the chin with an uppercut.

Thunk!

Backwards I went, arms pin-wheeling in an effort to keep the balance my brain had temporarily forfeited. Flop! My butt hit the mat. I squawked in anger.

Motherfucker.

Torres' fans roared. The ref counted. Eddy started cursing. All really bad signs. I took a few deep breaths and concentrated on the ref. He focused clearly in my vision so I got up, shrugged my shoulders and rolled my neck, bounced on my toes. I took my standing eight-count to recover, then nodded to the ref that I was ready to continue.

Nodded that I was ready to murder. Oh, baby. She

would pay for that one.

The ref told me to walk to him, rubbed my gloves on his shirt, got out of the way. "Box!" he said.

I launched a series of jabs that backed her into the ropes. She tried to pivot and counter, but I anticipated the angle and dropped down below it, throwing a steaming right-hand into her stomach, immediately stepping with my left foot to throw a hook. She clinched to catch her breath, grabbing my arms, then tried to sneak in another uppercut. I blocked it with my right glove, reached up and grabbed the back of her head with my left and pulled down. Instinctively, she raised her head to pull away, wasting precious energy and prolonging her recovery. I held her.

Ha!

"You can call me Herpes, bitch," I spat at her. "Because I always come back."

She didn't like that very much.

Growling in pain and anger, she struggled loose and sprang off her back foot with a wild four-punch combination that I danced away from, landing jabs on her forehead. Snapped a wicked right-cross that landed with a satisfying smack on her cheek, the crowd echoing it with a collective "Oooh..."

How you like me now?

Ding! The ref jumped between us and pointed to our corners. The crowd was on its feet cheering and clapping raucously. We raised our gloves to acknowledge the fans' support as we walked to our respective corners, our Teams already in the ring, waiting.

Eddy propped the stool on the mat and tore me a new one as soon as I sat down. "What the hell were you doing?! You abandoned the fight plan! I know you're smarter than that. When a jackass brays at you, you don't bray back! You trick him into carrying your load! Stop being stupid and listen!" he bellowed right in my face. His breath smelled like peanuts, but it felt like fire. The angry passion he emanated was super scary. Realizing how bad I had fucked up, all I could do was nod vigorously and agree to get back on the game plan.

"Yes, Coach!"

"I told you. When she wants to punch, you box! Get it through your thick head, girl! Box!"

"Yes, Coach!"

"Remember: weave, hook, weave, hook! Trick her with the right, then hook!"

"Yes, Coach!"

"You got knocked down, so you lost that round. You better not lose another to this girl."

"Yes, Coach!"

He ducked under the ropes, the cut man smeared Vaseline over my eyes and cheekbones, put my mouthpiece in. I stood. The bell rang.

Ding! Round two.

My ponytail, tank top, and trunks were soaked, sweat pouring off of me as if I were standing in a steam room. A towel flashed between my legs, wiping up the puddle I had left from my sixty-second break. My cheeks were beginning to throb, the jaw muscles inflamed from absorbing that bomb Torres had nailed on my chin. Motherfucker would be sore as hell later.

Super-duper.

I made a conscious effort to clear my head and focus on nothing, an illusion of elsewhere that erased all emotion from my body and allowed my muscles direct connection with my instincts, the muscle-memory that was programmed with Eddy's custom pugilistic software. Thinking slows a fighter down, inhibiting the mind-muscle connection with unnecessary pulses of information. Like spam, all in the damn way. Acting without thought or emotion is the recipe for speed.

And you know what they say about speed... It kills.

Torres darted in like a jackhammer, jab pumping as her feet pumped across the Tecate logo towards me. Right-hand cocked. I slipped the jabs, staying right in her face and watching for her right as she watched for mine. Let her chase me around the ring for a minute while I got into position for a counter punch. She kept coming straight at me, relentless, homing in, being the aggressor as part of her strategy to impress the judges and gain favor in the event that the fight went the distance. Aggressor is the only role she knows, a Mexican style of fighting she was taught, and taught well. Problem is, it's one-dimensional, all attack with little defense or counter punching involved. She would be in serious trouble if the roles suddenly reversed. That's why she's good at standing her ground and slugging. To prevent role-reversal, survival, protection of her style. I needed to hurt her to reverse it, get her out of her rhythm and off her game.

Hurt her bad.

With speed.

I pivoted the wrong way, seemingly by accident, as a result from frustration, let her chase me into a corner, raised my gloves to cover my head, elbows close together to cover my body. Pop-pop BAM! She wailed on my gloves and arms with a beautiful three-punch line drive. A half-second later, she reset and wailed again. This time I turned to the right and caught the third punch, a heavy right, on my left shoulder.

"Gaah!" I cried in feigned pain, grabbing her forearms and clinching. Having sensed my injury, she yanked up hard on my left arm, grunting sadistically, spraying spit and hot breath on my arms with the exertion. I cried out again, grabbed her elbow and pushed her to my left while pivoting to my right, spinning her into the corner, trading places. I backpedaled to the center of the ring, shaking out my arm and grimacing like my shoulder was torn or out of socket.

Torres paused in the corner and smiled at me. A green, white, and red flag of Mexico appeared behind her lips, a fierce grin representing the country she was kicking my ass for. "*Muerta, puta.*," you're dead, bitch, she said, bringing her gloves together in front of her face. She raised her Cleto Reyes and jabbed after me, explosive and feline, a lioness pouncing on her hamstringed prey.

Shame for her the prey wasn't really hamstringed.

Standing with my left arm hanging at my side, I stepped and weaved my head as if I actually believed I could slip her punches and fight with just my right arm. She came right at me with a one-two. I shifted onto my back foot to avoid her punches, her right brushed my nose. I stepped toward her with my left foot hard and quick, throwing my "useless" left arm up horizontally into a hook that had all of my legs, hips, and shoulders behind it, leverage and weight distribution in perfect textbook form.

Ka-Boom!

My glove hit her chin and I tightened up my fist, forearm and shoulder as it connected, solidifying it, driving it through the girl's face. Her head twisted, her eyes rolled, she flailed her arms reflexively, punches her brain triggered while forgetting to tell the rest of her that she was going down for a crash landing.

Flop!

Let the bodies hit the floor.

I stood over her, glaring, snarling, ignoring the referee who urgently motioned me to a neutral corner so he could count out my victim. But I didn't want him to count her out. I wanted her to get up so I could ride that roller coaster again. Feel that satisfying crunch of her jaw that made her eyes flash like flags of surrender.

The crowd was going mad from the action, feeling the blood lust and cheering the violent skill they had paid good money to witness, voicing their appreciation for not being disappointed.

Well, how about an encore?

"Get up, Torres!" I shouted at her. "You're not done yet. Get up!" Spit flew out of my mouth, drooling down my sweaty chin from lips that wouldn't seal properly around the mouthpiece, pink with tiny white bolts of lightning for teeth. The huge TV monitors showed me screaming at my inert opponent, shaking the glove that had knocked her down, spit and drool flowing from my snarl like a rabid dog.

Eddy's voice broke through the noise and my zone of rage. "Get your ass in that corner! Now! Shocker! Get your goddamn ass in that corner, girl!" he roared, spitting, snarling with even more rabid nature than I was.

Uh-oh.

Eddy cursing like that was a prequel to a dangerous event, a cataclysm on the brink of eruption. Hurry up and Run to Safety deal. I glanced around, expecting a mob of people to be running away from my coach's vicinity, listening for a siren to start blaring a warning. Remembering why I was suddenly scared, I trotted to a neutral corner, turned and watched the ref count, refusing to look at Eddy and his heated glare directed at me.

Torres was on one knee, slowly recovering from the extra seconds I had given her, staring at her gloves on the mat in front of her as her corner and her fans yelled and cheered encouragement to get up and fight. She stood, eyes wide and not completely focused, nodded to the ref. The ref told her to lift her gloves and step towards him. She did so without stumbling. He wiped her gloves on his shirt, asking if she was okay to continue. She nodded stoically, a true warrior's reaction, showing her people she wasn't a quitter and would fight on regardless of consequences to her health.

Gotta give it to the broad. She's a soldier. But she's still gonna be Shocker Victim #32.

The ref signaled us to continue. We raised our gloves.
Eddy yelled again, "Thirty-seconds! Get in her ass!"
Didn't have to tell me twice.

Torres was game and tried to work a few power punches
behind her jab. But I just bowled right over her, hammering
her into the ropes with hard, driving, blistering quick right-
hands that busted her nose and lips, spraying pink sweat all
over the mat and outside the ropes onto the Beautiful
People that sat nearest the ring. She bounded off the ropes
with a wild hook at my head. I ducked it, banged a right-
hand, left-hook to her stomach and ribs, springing up to
make it a double-hook to her head.

WHAM!

Sideways she went, grabbing the ropes for support. At
that point, the referee should have stopped the fight, but he
didn't.

And I wasn't mad about it.

Torres hit the corner post and covered up. I jumped in
and out at her, throwing a right-hand bomb every time my
weight came forward, rocking my monster, rocking her
head even though she caught the punches on her gloves.
Threw a ridiculously flashy over/under combination of
about ten blows, mostly ineffective, showboating my speed
demon to please the crowd. Torres fired back before the ref
TKO'd her for not defending herself. I paused and laughed,
relaxed my shoulders for a fraction of a second, launched
what I knew would be the *coup de grace.*

Right-hand, left-hook, right-hand, left-hook, over and
over, harder and faster, flowing, rocking Torres like a
bobble head dashboard toy. Switched, right-uppercut, left-
hook, over and under, upper-cutting between her elbows to
split her guard, tagging her chin, popping her head up
behind her gloves to meet my perfectly thrown hook.

Say hello to my little friend!
Crunch.

Ouch. That had to hurt.

My left glove compressed against her jaw, twisting her neck sharply, disrupting the flow of nerve impulses between her brain stem and spinal cord.

Incommunicado. Lights out.

Her eyes flashed surrender, her body dropped like a sniper had picked her off. The ref jumped in front of her, his back to me, waving his arms like he was doing jumping jacks. The fans were literally off their feet, jumping up and down screaming, spirit and spittle flying in joyful chaos. Someone grabbed my legs from behind and hoisted me above the people that flooded the ring with towels, cameras, and pumping celebratory fists. Eddy held me up on one shoulder like a trophy, his prize, a winner that made him a winner. I leaned sideways and kissed the top of his curly head.

Several officials in suits of grays and blues appeared in the twenty-foot squared circle, a sea of boxing's privileged locals, shuffling, pushing, turning through the throng to stand next to Eddy. He lowered me. My boots hit the mat and I looked up at huge men that lowered championship belts over me. One over my head, one around my waist. Eddy stood behind me and held the belts in place. The towering suits flanked us and a dozen cameras flashed, zoomed in. The TV monitors showed the WBC and WIBF world championship belts wrapped around an emotional girl that was visibly relinquishing the killer instinct in the form of tears. The giants surrounding me were blocking the view for most of the fans so Eddy lifted me again, slowly rotating me, his trophy holding her trophies. I basked in their adoration for what I knew would be the final time, tears pouring like sweat, smiling and sobbing, trying to breathe through my emotionally constricted throat.

I kissed Eddy's head again and choked out, "We did it, Coach."

He patted my leg. "You better believe it."

He lowered me, hugged me. Grabbed the belts I shrugged out of and looped them over a huge arm like bracelets. Flicked out a knife and cut off my gloves. I waded through the suits and media, ignoring the microphones shoved in my face, until I saw Team Torres jackets. My opponent's people saw me and made way so I could hug my no-longer enemy. I raised her hand. Cameras zoomed in. The TV monitors showed two serious combat women acknowledging respect for each other's lethal skills in battle. I hugged her again. Hugged her trainer. Waded back to Eddy.

And started sobbing harder. It was all over.

Forever.

"Let's get out of here, darling," Eddy said, wrapping a protective arm around me. He marched us through the suits and pursuing media like a cruise ship plowing through small waves.

PART IV

THE FLIGHT from Philadelphia to Atlanta was uneventful, other than the event that began inside of me. An anti-climax that happens immediately after every fight. I've never experimented with drugs, but I know what it feels like to be seriously high, to soar above everything and everybody and never want to come down.

I know what it feels like to come down, hard, a vertical drop without declinating in gradients. No levels of descent to get the body sensitized to running on less Go-Go Juice. Just an abrupt loss, a snatching, a dream life lost and never to be lived again.

And I know what it feels like to want more. To fiend for another hit.

I was in agonizing withdrawal when Eddy and I changed planes and landed at Gulfport International an hour later. My home was close by, in Biloxi, about a fifteen-minute drive. Ace picked me up in his Dodge Ram. We said our goodbyes to Eddy and he drove us home in silence. My man understood that I needed this time to think and readjust to being human again after playing the super hero role in the ring. Emotional decompression. Ace was lucky this process worked with me. Otherwise I'd have him on a steady diet of Ms. Bad Bitch, with liberal servings of Wicked Narcissism on the side, and, perhaps, served up on a lovely platter of I Run This Shit.

And feed it to him for breakfast, lunch, and dinner. So I fought for decompression. He stayed quiet.

And lucky.

We exited Interstate-10 in Woolmarket, in northern Biloxi, and turned onto Woolmarket Road. Headed east for about a quarter mile before turning into our driveway. A two-hundred foot steel building sat on five acres of grass surrounded by pine trees and residential streets behind it. The building had a granite stone front, dark blue steel sides, and a white roof with half a dozen skylights showing on the front, with more on the other half of the building.

Huge windows with awnings on the front entrance were dark, reflecting the streetlights. A large blue and gray sign stood guard at the left of the gravel drive, ten feet of fiberglass and wood, a tattooed chick bending over and reading the side of a door on a hot rod. The door advertised that this was a united business: Tattoology, my high-tech tattoo studio. And Custom Ace, the all-purpose mechanic shop that I renamed after marrying Alan "Ace" Carter.

We got out of the truck and were greeted by crickets that one by one started up their violin wings again once the Viper engine stopped growling at them. A dry breeze brought the fragrances of dozens of flowers and weeds that were blooming all over the yard. The smell of home, the ultimate aromatherapy. I walked inside, passing through the tattoo studio area and into a hallway that led to the auto shop in the back. The studio's lobby, office, and partitioned parlor were spotless, furnished with state-of-the-art equipment, and smelled similar to a hospital. Ace took my hand and we walked up the wooden stairs in the center of the hallway, into our home over the top of the studio.

I was struggling in a strange daze. An empty, numb, and wanting sensation that had nothing to do with jet lag. I was too spaced out to seriously analyze myself, but was sure the feeling is what others experience from traumatic loss. Like when a family member dies. A brother or sister, a twin, and you feel like you've lost a part of yourself.

A part of myself.

I could still hear the crowd cheering as I left the ring. Could still hear the roaring, vibrating echo that was the hypodermic for my Invincible dope, as I sat in the locker room, sobbing, as Eddy cut off my hand wraps and my promoter hustled the media that crowded in after us. I could still feel it happening...

But it wasn't happening. And never would again. I just didn't want to let it go. It didn't want to let me go, either.

Let her go.

Shocker Ares. She's gone.

I'm gone. I'm there. Now I'm here. Without her.

A part of myself.

"Are you okay, Clarice?" Ace asked, stroking my hair. He knew how much I loved that. And it helped, was soothing on so many levels. We sat in our comfy living room, in a huge leather chair that was our favorite spot because we could view the room and the artwork on the walls, the Turkish rugs that checkered the hardwood floor.

Mostly earth tones, the ambience was tranquilizing until your eyes wandered onto the mythological paintings dwelling like three-dimensional beings on the walls. Dragons, gods, and goddesses. Eight life-sized paintings with layered backgrounds and such strikingly realistic features that they seemed to lift off of the canvases and reach into your imagination. Monsters from the sea and the land, myths and legends that were created and accepted as real in every day life thousands of years ago. I painted them once I knew I was going to be building a home. Kind of like a home warming gift to myself, a series my Greek ancestors would surely appreciate.

A low moon white ceiling with small fluorescent spotlights lit up parts of the room and the paintings behind the sofas and our chair. The skylights were trimmed in dark blue, even darker now because of the night sky's lack of illumination. The forty-foot square floor was dark shiny wood with rugs in geometric patterns, though there were settings of furniture as well. A circular white leather sofa cornered a large flat screen TV and stereo entertainment center to our right. Tall corner windows with beige and white curtains were behind it and six-foot Apollo and Aphrodite renderings were on the far side of the windows. A small glass coffee table held remotes and coasters in front of the sofa. Behind that and almost directly across from us on one reddish-brown wall was another sofa. Long and white brushed leather with dark red throw pillows. A behemoth dragon on the wall above it floated in the air the entire length of the sofa, blowing flames on a tiny village far below its muscular wings, furious. Twin glass tables flanked it with red lamps and more coasters.

Behind us was another six-foot painting, this one with the goddess of the moon, Artemis. She was hunting for something, though I left that up for the observers' interpretation. Honestly, I didn't know what the hell the ancient broad was hunting for. So I didn't put it in the painting. But it looked kickass over our chair.

The chair had the appearance and feeling of a king's throne, with an aura of cunning emitting from the scenes of sprites and fairies carved into the thick oak legs and arms, the little creatures twisted around each other erotically, expressions of carnal magic that seemed to honor a superior being. Like it was crafted so Conan and his concubines could have an orgy on it. Maybe I should paint that and hang it over the chair...

I'm leaned back against my man and sighed, closed my eyes. Then remembered he had asked me a question. "I know I'm being a drama queen. I'm having issues here," I said by way of apology.

"Just relax and tell me when you feel like it," he murmured, wanting no part of Ms. Bad Bitch. Wanting to stay lucky.

That made me smile. "Relax? What is that?"

"Shh. Don't do that. You know you'll feel better if you just talk it out," he murmured again, brushing his vibrating lips on the side of my neck, kissing it. He moved my hair and kissed my nape.

Oh, goddamn. The man knew how to get my mind out of the gutter, and off to frolic in a different kind of gutter. I started squirming, thinking of the Orgy Throne painting again. Giving it a title made it real in my mind, a fantasy, one I wanted to bring to life, lose myself in at this very moment.

"You're absolutely right," I whispered in a tight, I Have An Idea Voice. My tone rose louder, husky. "Let's talk this out. Come on. Get up. I need your help with something in our bedroom. Let's scream that motherfucker out." I stood and grabbed his wrists, snatched him out of the chair. I needed this, as a cleansing of sorts. Yeah, that felt right.

Yeah. And Nolan won't be here until 6 a.m., when Mom drops him off. Plenty of time to deal with this...

I gripped his arms tighter.

"Are you going to hurt me again?" he said with a little worry laced in it. But excitement, too. Like he was about to get back on a theme park ride that scared him stupid, but he kept getting back in line anyway.

"Probably so."

"That's cool."

He laughed nervously as I led him down the hallway to our bedroom.

PART V

Biloxi, Mississippi
March 21, 2010

MAIN STREET in Biloxi was a curious mix of life. The buildings of the numerous businesses were in as many variations of shapes, colors and sizes as the people that populated the area. A real potpourri of humanity. But there were clear distinctions between two elements, unmistakable patterns that contrasted one class from the other.

There were the legit folks, mostly overweight whites with some older blacks, Asians, and a few Latinos. They drove nice cars and wore nice clothes, walked and talked in a manner that proclaimed them as law-abiding citizens. The suspect crowd, mostly blacks, with groups of young Asians, Latinos and whites disseminated throughout the area, drove old hoopties that branded them as probable drug users, or rode in customized bling rides that screamed illicit gain. Their fashion tastes favored sports jerseys or tank tops to show off tattoos, sagging, baggy pants and huge boots with loose shoestrings, or basketball shoes in loud colors.

The legits waved, nodded, or were oblivious to the police cars that drove by, confident in their citizenship and showing no concern at being observed by law enforcement. The suspects pretended to be oblivious, mostly unsuccessfully, by suddenly finding something to make them look busy or show they had a completely legal purpose for their present actions. Behavior that suggested the potential to break rules and a lot of guilt on their collective conscience.

"Look at that guy over there," Jimmy said, pointing at a young black man that had obviously been up all night. The teenager's pants were dropped below his butt, showing red boxers and a Tommy Hilfiger logo. The hustler saw the cop car and automatically pulled up his pants, an unconscious response that was nearly instinctual among street thugs because it made them a target for the boys in blue. "Jerkoff could at least wear clean drawers, you know? I mean, look at his ass. It looks like a fucking bruised apple. Who wants to see that?"

"I don't get it either," Hector replied, chuckling. "Personally, I don't mind the saggy thing. Makes them easier to catch." They shared a laugh. "One time, I chased an Asian kid through his house and into his backyard. He made it about fifty feet before his pants fell around his ankles and tripped him. Dummy busted himself."

"Oh, yeah! I remember that." The car swelled with loud belly laughter. They pointed out more suspects with bloopers potential as they prowled the dawning neighborhood. Some of the people were so obviously up to no good that they panicked and fled at first glimpse of the patrol. The guffaws continued, with wheezing, coughs and tear-welled eyes.

"Hey, Jimmy. They are like little raccoons with their robbers' masks, right?" Hector choked out between laughs.

"We caught them with their paws in the trash and they ran back into the woods! Yeah!" Jimmy exclaimed, wheezing and executing a few unplanned swerves.

The street light timers sensed the presence of the sun, blinking off the lights and erasing that eerie yellow-orange color that predominates night activity hues in cities. A glare in the eyes that made the sky and buildings less distinguishable, and hid most of the ugliness of concrete and people alike. It was morning. The illuminating glow of the rising sun chased away the cloaking shadows to reveal the true nature of the area in all its glory: Filthy. Ugly. With random symmetry and appeal. Wrinkles, cracks, and dirt became more visible on the faces of stores and the people that walked into them.

"He should have called by now," Jimmy said, switching into the left lane without the courtesy of a blinker.

"Who, El Maestro?" Hector asked.

"Yeah, who else? I thought you said he would call by now."

"He said he would text. And to be on Main Street at sunup. We're here. I don't know what to tell you, Jimmy."

"Great. Just fucking great. What kind of an organized crime boss is he, huh? Can't keep a fucking appointment with his security team. I swear, these greaser-"

"Wait a minute, Jimmy. Just got a text." Hector's phone finished its chime as he took it from a compartment on his gun belt. He flipped open the purple Samsung, read the message. "It's him. He says to pull over the green Chevy Cruze in front of us."

"What the hell?" Jimmy leaned forward with his head over the steering wheel, squinting ahead into the shadowed traffic, searching through the people hurrying to work or school. He spotted the car and maneuvered to get behind it. Hit the lights for a routine traffic stop. "Is this him?"

"I think so."

"Be ready for anything."

"I know," Hector acknowledged, unsnapping his gun.

The Cruze pulled over to the right side of the road, stopping in front of a dress shop with mannequins in the windows displaying wedding gowns. The driver parked and waited without movement, both hands on top of the wheel.

Jimmy got out, blasts of wind from passing cars tugged at the door, assaulting his nose and lungs with smog particulates. He coughed and wheezed. Unsnapped and drew his gun. Held it against his leg as he approached the back of the green Cruze. Horns honked at an intersection nearby. Tiny rocks tinkled against the police cruiser from churning tires as a duo of dump trucks rumbled by. Hector approached the car from the passenger side.

The driver rolled down both windows simultaneously. "Hector. Jimmy. I think I would feel more pleasure from seeing you if you weren't holding drawn guns," greeted El Maestro. Clean and trim in a blue Nautica button-up with gold sailboats all over it, his light brown skin and black chin beard looked deceptively young on a man in his late sixties. The short dark hair on top with specks of gray, bald spot showing through, were the only indications of his age. He smiled, showing teeth as bright as his watch and rings.

"Good to see you, El Maestro," Hector said, holstering his gun.

"Yeah, as always," Jimmy agreed, still holding his gun and glancing in all directions.

El Maestro looked down at the weapon, back to Jimmy's nervous face. He said, "You seem overly anxious. Do you not trust me anymore? Or have you a guilty conscience about something?"

"It's not that," Jimmy replied, forcing himself to calm down, stop looking so paranoid. "We're a security team. I'd prefer to stay ready for anything."

"So you've heard, then."

"Yeah. We heard about Jose," Hector said. "Big news at the station yesterday."

El Maestro turned to Hector. "A victory for law enforcement, certainly. Jose was a warrior with status, and has been wanted for over a decade now. He will be remembered for his loyalty to La Familia and his sacrifices for his countrymen," he said, voice beginning to break with emotion. He cleared his throat. "I want you to investigate his death. Find out who did this and you will be rewarded."

"Any idea who did it?" Jimmy inquired, staring El

Maestro in the face without blinking.

He didn't respond right away. Looked down to gather himself. Turned to the right, locking eyes with Hector. "Traitors," El Maestro growled. Hector jumped as if accused. Jimmy brought his gun up and pointed it at the back of El Maestro's head. "It was traitors," he continued, unaware of the instrument of death aimed at his cranium. "Somebody from inside the organization. Either La Familia or one of the associates or security teams," he told Hector without a blink, passion and anger smoldering in his eyes.

Jimmy lowered the gun behind him. Glanced around to see if anyone was gawking. There wasn't. He wheezed out a breath he didn't realize he was holding.

"Traitors?" Hector turned his head sideways, hoping to appear thoroughly confused. "Who? Who do we investigate?"

"If I knew you wouldn't be investigating. It happened in your district. There are only so many people linked to us that could have arranged a meeting with Jose. Find out the 'who' and eliminate them. If you need reinforcements, you know where to find me," he said, looking back to Jimmy.

"We'll take care of it. As soon as we know anything Hector will text you," Jimmy assured him.

"Excellent. We must show our enemies that we don't let transgressions go unpunished." He looked over at Hector. "And we must show our family that vengeance will be pursued. Pronto."

Hector just stared back, speechless. His eyes flickered to Jimmy like a plea for help.

"El Maestro," Jimmy said, calling his attention away from his partner, who now had a near confessional look of guilt controlling his face. "You said we would have a detail today. Where are the mules? Let's take care of business."

"You are right, of course," he replied, taking a phone from his pocket. He texted a quick note, pressed SEND. "Let us not waste time chatting of unimportant matters."

"El Maestro, I don't think he meant −" Hector began, but was silenced by an upraised hand.

"I know what he meant. And we are wasting time. That car," he said, pointing at a late-model white Pontiac GTO that had pulled over to the opposite side of the road fifty yards ahead of them, "is your security assignment. Instead of the usual switch-off in Gulfport, I had the Hancock County team escort them here. All switch points will be changed randomly from now on. Follow them north and you will receive a text with the next switch point." He opened the center console, removed a gray Nokia cell phone and handed it to Hector. "Your new phone. I now have a GPS app that shows me where all my security teams are, so coordination will be more efficient."

"Okay, still business as usual. We'll take care of it," Jimmy said, pretending he wasn't unnerved by the additional security. Dammit, he thought. I'll have to figure out a way around this tracking and random switch point shit now. He holstered his gun, grimacing, walked back to the patrol car.

El Maestro turned to Hector. "Find the person who is behind this betrayal, Hector. Kill them. I will personally make sure your family in Juarez benefits from your dedication to La Familia. Good deeds earn great honor, *hermano*."

Hector didn't reply, just stared after the green sedan as it pulled into traffic and turned its lights off, the morning air brightening.

Sea gulls cawed overhead, grabbing Hector's attention, the sound like an omen of consequence. He stared up at the scavengers, eyes glazing, mystified.

His heart quickened.

A premonition sneaked its way into his thoughts, like a diseased mouse squeezing through a tight crack and entering a room that had never before been invaded by an infectious entity. The realization that he was a traitor as well as a dirty cop did not sit well in his mind. Uncoordinated from looking up, he stumbled to the side. Looked down at the concrete and his boots. To the left at the patrol car.

Jimmy stuck his head out of the driver's side window. "What the fuck are you doing? Let's go, let's go!" he yelled, pointing at the Pontiac up the street like Hector was a deaf dummy that needed blunt, elementary gestures to comprehend his meaning.

Hector hurried to the car, got in, and they pulled into traffic. Made a U-turn to get behind the GTO and followed them to the interstate.

"What the hell was that all about? What did El Maestro say?" Jimmy wanted to know. He divided his attention between driving and trying to analyze his friend.

"He just said he would take care of my family if we found the traitor." He shrugged.

"And what did you say?"

"Nothing."

"You didn't say anything?"

"I just said I didn't. What's your problem?" Hector scowled at him, clearly getting upset.

"Nothing, nothing. I'm sorry. I'm just a little stressed. I almost shot El Maestro a few minutes ago. Look, forget it, okay? Let's focus on the job. You know those guys?" he asked, indicating the two men in the GTO.

"No. Don't think so."

"Wonder how much product is stashed in that car. Probably a million worth, at least," he speculated. They drove in silence until they reached the on-ramp to Interstate-10 West, which would take them to Highway 49 North. Jimmy tapped his meaty hands on the steering wheel. "Hey, how'd he get the name the Teacher, anyway."

"He really is a teacher," Hector answered, watching the

woods that lined the side of the interstate. He didn't look at his partner, hoping Jimmy would take the hint that he didn't feel like talking.

He didn't catch on. "No shit? From where?"

"University in Juarez. Economics and commerce professor."

"Commerce, huh? Yeah, that makes sense. No wonder that guy's like a fucking secret agent or something. Controlling a drug commerce relay race by using our government's own security structure to facilitate it. That GTO is the baton, and we are the runners that have to pass it off to the next runner."

"It's brilliant, *ese*," Hector said, grudgingly becoming interested in the conversation. "No cop would think to pull over a car another cop is already following. And buying a cop or two in every county on the route is cheaper than losing shipments and drivers to law enforcement. It's nearly foolproof."

"Nearly," Jimmy agreed. "But I don't plan on passing these fucking batons much longer, brilliant or otherwise. I've done my tour of duty, Hector." He patted the badge on his chest. "For both sides of the fence."

They fell silent again. Another mile passed and the GTO pulled over to the side in the emergency lane, hazard lights flashing.

"What the fuck?" Jimmy roared, slowing and pulling in behind them. "Be ready." He unsnapped his gun. Shifted into PARK and opened his door.

A slim Latino of medium height in his early forties stepped out of the Pontiac, loose fitting white pants and peach pastel shirt fluttering like flags as cars sped by. He shouted back at the patrol car. "Something's wrong with the *coche!*" he hollered over the din.

"What's the matter?" Jimmy yelled back. Stuck a fist to his mouth, coughed several times.

"The dash lights are going *loco*! And the car is losing power! *No se*," he said.

Jimmy stuck his head back in the car. "Hector you know more about cars than me. Check it out while I cover you."

"I'll take a look," he said, sighing. He opened the door, got out and walked to the white sports car. Asked the driver to step aside, sat in the seat and turned the key on.

Jimmy stood behind his door, hand on gun, watching the trees lining the side of the interstate and the cars approaching that may suddenly stop and sprout enemy targets. His energy abruptly failed him, dipping so low his knees nearly buckled and dropped him where he stood. Tiny dark spots appeared in his vision, little black holes that sucked in the light and matter in their vicinity. He leaned on the door, scowling viciously as he recovered.

All this damn greaser stress, he thought. Motherfuckers are determined to put me in the ground before I get a chance to get out. I'll have to get stronger blood pressure meds this week.

Fuck!

Hector trotted back to the cruiser. He and his partner ducked into their sides, closed the doors. "I don't know what the problem is, maybe something electrical. It will still drive, though. I gave them directions to a shop in Woolmarket. Only one exit away."

"You're talking about Custom Ace, right? Good idea. They're fast."

"Hopefully, it's only a minor problem and we'll be back on the road before lunch."

"Has anybody replaced Jose?"

"Don't think so. El Maestro mentioned that new GPS app, so I think he's running the show until someone gets promoted to lieutenant."

"So we report this directly to El Maestro. Text him a report. We'll park down the road from Custom Ace and stay on point."

"Sounds good, Jimmy." Hector took the Nokia out of his belt.

PART VI

Biloxi, Mississippi
March 21, 2010

THE ALARM CLOCK went off and we awoke to the Kings of Leon belting out *Sex on Fire*. Last night's experience ran through my head in vivid emotion and I started laughing. Ace obviously had the same thoughts because he was laughing and singing along as he got out of bed.

"*Your sex is on fire!*" he sang, playing air guitar and stepping around the room like he was performing for a crowd. Except a guitar wasn't what he was slinging around. He had absolutely no butt, and his narrow hips made his penis seem comically out of proportion. Like it could eat peanuts out of my hand.

I laughed harder.

He turned to look at me. "What?" he said, like him playing naked air guitar shouldn't be that funny.

"Nothing. It's just that, well, did you eat Corn Flakes as a kid?" I asked with a big-eyed innocent look, already knowing the answer. I sat up. The blanket fell down, exposing my chesticles. Peekaboobie.

Ace looked at them and waggled his eyebrows. "Corn Flakes? Nope."

"Oh, that's right. You ate Noassatall Flakes." I looked at his hips. "Gigantic bowls of it."

"Hey, who needs a butt when you got this?" he responded, holding his "this" in both hands and playing a solo on it. "Your sex is on fire!" he jammed, dancing around again. He was really getting into it, whipping it up and down like Hendrix at Woodstock.

I laughed so hard my eyes had rivers pouring out at all corners. I wanted to spend the rest of my life right here, feeling this exquisite joy. "Oh man, that's good stuff." I wiped my eyes. "You won't win any mainstream talent shows, but I think you have a bright future in adult comedy. Let's set up a stage with tiki torches. We'll put on grass skirts and I'll drum on your coconut knees while you play your instrument."

He stopped and gave me a look of interest, like he was considering my joke as a serious idea. Then he frowned and shook his head. "It won't work."

"And why is that?"

"We would need a bass player. A bass guitar is bigger than a regular guitar. Where are we going to find a bigger guitar than mine?" he said, face serious again, gesturing at his crotch like it was the tallest skyscraper in the world.

"And the ego has landed." A fit of giggles grasped me and I lay back on the bed. Oh man, that's good stuff. I sat up again. "I could get a strap-on, but the competition might-"

"And we would need a singer," he interrupted, pretending he hadn't heard the solution to finding something bigger. He turned and walked to the bathroom, the sight of his no-butt dropping me back on the bed giggling once more. He gave it a smack, then yelled, "And you can't sing!" The shower turned on.

I jumped up, laughter cutting off instantly. "I can too sing!" I yelled back, a little girl in a My Daddy Can Beat Up Your Daddy argument. I stormed into the bathroom, slammed the door, tagged Ace with a quick combo to the body that knocked him off his feet in the tub. He fell, flailing his arms and ripping the shower curtain off the rod, thumped down on his no-butt. Water cascaded from the showerhead, bouncing off his legs, sprinkling on the floor. The Giggle God struck me down again and I tumbled into the tub with the cute jerk.

Our bedroom was quiet, dark, with the comforting aromas of hygiene products and natural scents that accumulated from a couple's active life. It was our sanctuary, a chamber with no technology to distract us from sleeping. As a fighter, I've studied the science of the body, so I know how important quality sleep is for recouping sharpness in the nervous system, for mental and physical keenness. Deep sleep is important for so many bodily functions. So that's all we do in here.

Well, and play air guitar.

The bed was large, low to the floor with white pillows against a black wooden headboard, huge white comforter, rumpled, hanging half off the mattress onto the gray-carpeted floor. The thirty-foot square room had dark blue and white walls, two dressers with mirrors, black wood, and a small walk-in closet. Relatively bare bones.

Wide awake from our energizing shower, we quickly dressed in our work clothes. I really didn't care for traditional mechanic's uniforms of dark blue. That's all good for shops that service factory cars, or whatever. But a custom shop like we run is highly artistic, and I believe our uniforms should show more style than the usual, boring attire.

So, I got with a friend that sews for a living. We designed Custom Ace and Tattoology uniforms with a blue camouflage base. Blue, gray, and white deals. The mechanics have combat-type pants with Custom Ace logos on the side cargo pockets, and zip-up tops with logos on the back. There were plenty of random sized pockets and matching mechanic's gloves. My top has a MIG welding machine for a name badge backdrop with CLARICE in wicket tribal letters. Ace had a diagnostic machine name badge, our painter had a spray gun, and so on, each employee labeled with his specialty.

My tattoo artists, who will open the studio after noon,

have blue camo shorts for the guys, a skirt for the counter girl/manager, and tank tops to show off their tatts while advertising Tattoology on the front.

You know the famous statue of soldiers raising the American flag on Iwo Jima? Our Custom Ace logo is soldiers raising a wrench. The Tattoology logo is soldiers raising a tattoo machine. The colors match the building and go with a theme that we are soldiers of creation.

Bring in any tatt idea or car idea you can imagine. Our soldiers will create it.

Down the stairs we went. The thick cedar wood lacked the creaks and squeaks that plague older steps. The sheetrock walls were dark blue and bare except for a huge Avatar movie poster halfway down on the right. The only light was a black light overhead that made the Avatar's eyes and skin glow with unnatural blues and greens. T-gel shampoo drifted up from my man's freshly scrubbed hair. He paused at the poster, turned his face up to me and did an uncanny impression of the Avatar. Mouth wide, eyes large and glowing. He grinned. His teeth glowed green.

We stepped off the stairs into the hallway. Turned right, walked through a heavy steel door that insulated the tatt parlor from most of the incredible racket we made banging on cars. Ace held the door for me, a perfect gentleman, closed it with a click of the latch and snip of pressurized air, sealing the quieter half of the building.

He inhaled. "I love the smell of diagnostic machines in the morning," he announced, eyes closed, smiling.

"I hate to tell you, Bread Stick, but that's the smell of burnt diagnostics this morning," rumbled a black man in a blue camo suit, walking up to us, cleaning his hands on a rag. BOBBY stood out from a paint spray gun on his name badge. Taller than Ace and a hundred pounds heavier, he looked and sounded like Ving Rhames, if Ving looked like he just stepped off the Mr. Olympia stage. All Bobby needed was posing trunks and oil.

"Uh. Okay. When you say 'burnt' ..." Ace said, looking at Bobby like a kid who was just told his favorite pet had been murdered.

"Burnt means just that. When I opened the shop and turned the equipment on, your girlfriend growled and spit sparks at me. The transformer circuit is blacker than I am," Bobby said bluntly, smiling at the look of pain that took hold of Ace's face.

The poor guy ran off towards his machine yelling, "Daddy's coming!"

"No running in the shop, you idiot!" I yelled after him, grinning.

"Now that was some funny shit," Bobby told me. He stood with hands on waist, staring at his running friend with a big silly smile.

I looked at his arms. They were as big as my torso. "What?" I said.

"His face. That geek really thinks those machines are his babies."

"They are," I defended my guy. "He created them, gave them life." I patted the soldiers and wrench logo on Bobby's side pocket.

"If you say so, Boss," he rumbled, smiling and walking back to his work station, a paint booth surrounded by tables full of paint and body tools. His chuckle sounded like a 500hp CAT engine.

I did my morning inspection. Walked from station to station to make sure the apprentices had cleaned and organized the tools last night, and also to check on the progress of various projects. Everything looked spectacular.

The shop was a hundred-and-fifty feet long and one-hundred feet wide, with six bays and five car lifts. Huge red and black Craftsman tool boxes towered next to the lifts, with black air hoses snaking down from the ceiling and around the boxes to rest on metal work tables. Pneumatic tools and bench vises on one table drew my eye. Certain tools have the ability to intrigue me on sight. To attract my interest with their scents of petroleum, amazing geometry and unique capabilities. Each station had a mélange of oils and degreasers that glistened from forged steel, twinkling with the promise of lighting up the innovative half of my brain, if only I'd stop and pick something up.

I swear I could feel it tingling right now. Or maybe that was just the fumes.

The twenty-foot ceiling with I-beams overhead held rolling electric wenches that we used for everything from lifting car engines to holding an employee upside down for a birthday spanking. We even had Bobby's big ass up there one day.

A grinder suddenly clicked on with an air whine, buzzing a wire wheel on metal. The 20hp air-compressor added to the racket, cranking up its thump-pump to replenish pressure in the reservoir. Bobby, standing in front of an old Chevy with a clear face shield strapped around his muscular head, ground rust from a bumper, sparks fanning spectacularly.

A white Pontiac GTO drove up to the side of the shop. I guessed it to be a 2005 model, factory spec, but still kickass. I motioned for them to pull into an empty garage bay. The two men in the car waved and nodded, backed up and drove the Goat into the shop, rattles and clangs from one seriously disgruntled drive-train reverberating loudly. I winced, looking at the poor car with a feeling that put a heavy frown on my face. God, like seeing a sick animal that would be a wondrous beauty if someone would just mother it. I wanted to give this car some TLC, a quirk I indulge every time high-end wheels rolled in here.

At this point I should warn you. I am an auto racist. If you bring your Kia in here, I'm not going to feel sad and want to mother it. I'll probably point at it and laugh. Fair warning.

I walked over to Bobby, who had put aside his work to attend to the customers. He was explaining a delay and technical problem to the two men who stood in front of their car looking like characters from Miami Vice, white dress pants, pastel shirts, and all.

"... but the diagnostic specialist is here now," Bobby said, nodding toward Ace, the muttering nerd with dozens of colored wires strewn over his lap, shoulders, head inside a huge machine. "He'll fix the machine in no time and we'll scan your car for the problem."

"We need the car working by lunch, *senor*," the guy in the peach pastel said to Bobby, looking nervous about something. Possibly intimidated by Bobby's presence. Lots of customers were. "We have an important meeting we cannot miss. I will pay you double if you will hurry, *por favor*."

Bobby's eyes widened just a tad at the mention of a double payment. He blinked and I heard, cha-ching! "I understand, sir, and we will do that for you. But we have to wait –"

"Bobby, don't sweat it," I said. "I'll take care of these guys. Have to do it the old fashioned way, but hey, these gentlemen are offering incentive for the effort." I smiled at them. "First-class service for two first-class gentlemen." Pay us double? Go to the front of the shop, sirs. They smiled back, relieved, stroked by my charm, happy that they would make their meeting on time. I could sense they were seriously scared of missing it, and were willing to go to great expense to avoid that fate.

Hmm... Something felt off here. Wrong.

Two Mexican dudes with deep pockets of cash, a boss car, going to a meeting of serous consequence.

Doesn't take a genius to figure this one out. Drug guys.

Swell.

"*Gracias, senora.* We cannot thank you enough," Peach Pastel said, speaking formal, audio taped-learned English without contractions.

I looked at Turquoise Pastel, wondering if he could speak any English at all. Looked back at Peach, smiling. "Hey, we believe in customer service. You guys be sure to bring this baby back for an upgrade. With a supercharger and a little electronics package, this Goat could have the power of five-hundred horses."

"We will consider it, *senora. Gracias,*" he said, beaming.

I knew they wouldn't return for my suggestion, but I beamed back anyway, thinking it was a good idea to be courteous to men who could potentially turn into villains from a Don Johnson show. "Looking forward to it. You can wait in the lounge if you like." I pointed to the hall entrance. "Walk through that door there and go into the parlor to the right. There are computers with Internet, video games and free coffee. Help yourself, guys."

"*Gracias,*" they both said, smiling and heading to the lounge. The heavy snip of the door closing was masked by the running grinder once again wielded by Bobby, the biggest rust racist on the planet.

I opened the driver's side on the GTO and sat in the leather seat. Gave it a squirm. Weird, hard, didn't agree with me. Turned the key to start the engine. It turned over, idling roughly and shaking the whole car, the view behind me blurred in the mirrors. It had oil pressure and wasn't overheating so I left it running, stepped out, grabbing a multi-meter from a toolbox. Got back in and ducked under the dashboard to find the fuse box. Used the meter to make sure the fuel pump and ignition were getting the juice they needed.

Everything was in spec so I crawled out from under the steering wheel and turned the key off. Pulled the hood release. As I pushed off the seat to stand up, I noticed the carpet around the base of the seat wasn't aligned properly. Looked closer and discovered that someone had removed this seat before, possibly to access the ECU, the main computer that was bolted under the seat.

Hmm. Maybe something on the wiring harness vibrated loose or wasn't installed properly.

I jumped out, grabbed an air ratchet and speed-rack of sockets. Ducked back in and unbolted the seat like I was on an Indy Car pit crew, pneumatic ratchet buzzing. The fantasy pit crew radio chatter I voiced should have made me feel silly. But it didn't. Foolishness is normal for a woman that is getting acquainted with a manly beast such as this Pontiac. The seat base lifted off of the carpet and exposed the wiring harness, part of it smashed beneath it. The wires were grounding out on the metal rail. Looks like I found the problem.

Boo-yah! Now to business.

I pushed the seat over backwards to get some elbow room and noticed some seriously bad repair work on the base of the seat where the leather attached. "What upholstery hell is this?" I muttered at the terrible work. Who repaired this thing, Hillary Clinton? I mean, it was that bad. Like some hag with kindergartner skills crawled her mammoth behind in here, butchered the seat and scammed the owners.

Scammed... Shit. Drug guys. This seat was probably loaded with dope for their VIP meeting.

Just lovely.

"It's a beautiful morning," I sang to myself, a load of sarcasm topped with a healthy dose of oh-my-fucking-god.

What do I do? Report them? Pretend I never noticed? The How To Start A Small Business book I studied before opening this joint neglected to offer a solution for this particular situation. I couldn't just let these assholes go and have this shit land on the streets for kids like mine to snort and smoke and fuck up their lives.

A sickly chill pulsed in my stomach.

First things first. Calm down. And check it. It's entirely possible my intuition is wrong and this seat was victimized by someone who couldn't tell the difference between foam and sand when they repaired it.

I grabbed a serrated knife, made an incision where the plastic and foam joined. Cut a six-inch gap and stuck my little finger in. Felt something that wasn't supposed to be there.

"Nooo," I moaned. My stomached cranked up the sick feeling, jumped into another dimension with zero gravity and pterodactyls crashing around. Much worse than a case of nervous butterflies. This was getting bad really quickly. "Oh shit," I breathed, seriously not liking this unknown territory. I opened the gap a little more, took off my gloves, reached in and pulled out a duct-taped brick of dope. No wonder my squirm had been rejected. There must be six bricks of crap in this seat base.

I looked at the other seats, suddenly able to see with x-ray vision, bricks of dope crammed throughout every cushion in the car. "Oh shit," I stupidly said again. My heart started thumping harder, filling my ears, veins aching, as I thought about the risks involved in what I could or should do. These guys could have guns. Nolan would be down here any time. He usually explores the shop before going out front to the bus stop. I have to tell Ace and Bobby.

No.

They may act suspicious or get all protective if the drug dudes come back to check on their car.

Okay, lady. You can do this. Get it together here. Your family and employees are in danger, but you can still think straight. So stop being an idiot and just call the freaking cops.

Yeah. Then I'll act like I'm working on the car until they get here.

I unzipped a side pocket, took out my phone and dialed 9-1-1. Waited a hundred-thousand years for someone to answer. It rang once. "Nine-one-one emergency," chirped a professional female voice.

"There are drug runners at my mechanic shop. I'm working on their car right now and the seats are loaded with dope," I said in a low, rapid voice. My top pocket and collar vibrated from my heartbeat, palm sweaty on the phone.

"What's the address?

"Custom Ace on Woolmarket Road." I gave her the street number and hung up before she asked me to stay on the line or some nonsense. I needed to look busy here. I squatted down, put my phone away, then froze at a sound that was ridiculously unexpected in my present mental state.

A disturbing, haunted house laugh began in the back of the shop, over in Ace's corner of gadgets and contraptions. Starting low and throaty, Ace laughed higher and faster. His incredibly retarded but adorable mad scientist laugh. Damn thing caught me off guard every time he did it. He must have fixed the diagnostic machine.

"It's alive! IT'S ALIVE! Hoo-hoo-hoo ha-ha-ha," the crazy bastard trumpeted.

Well. There it is. Let's hope that madcap exhibition didn't attract-

"Dad! Dad, did you fix it?" Nolan asked, running into the shop. The hall door clunked closed behind him. He saw me, frowned, stopped running and walked like a good boy over to his father. The Khaki school uniform made him look mature only until the grease stains appeared. And they would. And I would have to clean them.

"Fuck," I grumbled, cursing grease stains and the entire situation in general. The day had started off great. What happened? I stared at the overturned car seat, distraught, indecisive. Scared and pissed off. I looked back at Nolan, mind racing.

"I heard your Fixed It laugh," Nolan told Ace.

"Yeah, my guy. I fixed it," Ace replied, bumping fists with him. They both wore identical Kool Aid smiles. I felt left out so I tried one on, but it literally shook off when I glanced at the brick of dope. Ace held something up. "See this wire?"

"Yep," Nolan confirmed.

"It's broken. It got too hot and melted. Grab a flathead screwdriver and unscrew this clamp. I'll show you how to replace a melted wire."

"I thought it was a 'faulty' wire," he said, smiling.

Ace bumped fists with him again. "You're too smart for me, son."

"Yeah, right!" He laughed. Opened the top drawer on a toolbox, rummaging around with pure glee.

Damn. Here come the stains.

Realizing my indecision was getting out of hand, I briefly considered if other people had weird thoughts in times of crisis. Like a shock buffer. Whatever it was, sitting here like an ignoramus was out of character for me. I've never been this passive under pressure. I needed to get that kid out of here, and do it without causing a panic or triggering a dramatic hissy fit worthy of a bad reality show.

Ugh. This could be harder than just going head-to-head with the Miami Vice villains.

With that prioritized thought, I stood to walk the Gauntlet of Nolan, but spun back the other way when the hall door opened.

"*Senora*, how bad is it?" Peach Pastel said, walking to the garage bay his car and mechanic occupied.

I took a calming breath and smiled at him. "Shouldn't be much longer now. I think I found the problem." I sized him up with a glance, reminding myself this wasn't boxing

with illegal punches, anything goes, zeroing in on possible
targets of chin, throat, abdomen, groin, knees, marking him
as an Enemy. Stepped over to him quickly, hoping to
distract him from seeing –

"The seat, *senora*. Is there a problem with it?" he said,
leaning into the open door, inspecting the cut I had made.

Boy, I sure felt dumb. Why didn't I reposition the seat?
That's one could'a-should'a-would'a that would haunt me
for the rest of my life.

He saw the duct taped brick on the floorboard. Then
drew an enormous silver revolver from under his shirt, eyes
narrowing as he brought it up to point at me.

Without thinking, I lunged forward and drilled him
with a lead-right.

~ ~ ~

"All available units, respond to distress call at Custom
Ace on Woolmarket Road..."

"*Hijo de puta!*" Hector exclaimed, staring at the radio
in surprised disbelief. "What happened, Jimmy?"

"Fuck, fuck! I don't know. But we'll be the first to find
out," Jimmy said, shifting the patrol car into DRIVE. "We'll
be there in two seconds. Maybe we can clean this mess up
before any other units arrive. Our priority is to protect the
cartel guys."

"All right. But no killing, okay? I can't take any more of
that."

"What? Who the fuck said anything about killing?" he
yelled, face reddening. He coughed several times. "Just
calm down. We don't know what's going on over there." He
floored the gas pedal, darting the car out onto the road, rear
tires spinning, squealing. The Custom Ace sign was visible
a quarter-mile up the road.

~ ~ ~

The air ratchet in my hand made my fist heavy and solid.
Lethal. I didn't just strike the guy, I hit his chin so hard his

head looked like it would twist off his neck. His owl impression lasted one second, his head twisted back straight, his knees buckled, crumpling him over the door. The gun dropped, clattering as he slid off the door and sprawled on the concrete awkwardly. His eyes danced epileptically before closing completely.

I stood over him, panting, excited. I've never hit anybody that hard before. A horseshoe-loaded boxing glove couldn't have executed a better knockout. Under different circumstances, this would have been a toe-curling aphrodisiac.

I took a deep breath, ignoring my curling toes that defied that last thought, reached down to grab the pistol.

And saw it kicked away by a very nice Perry Ellis dress shoe.

I followed the shoe up the leg of white pants to find the other Mexican dude, Turquoise Pastel, pointing a matching revolver in my face. "Oh shit," I said, my highly intelligent response of the day.

"*Senora*, please be calm. No one has to get hurt here. *Comprende?*" he said, squatting down and grabbing the gun off the floor. He stuck it in his waistband, eyeing me warily. He looked more scared than me. The flock of pterodactyls in my guts didn't agree with that assessment.

I held up my hands, peripherally noticing the air hose had somehow disconnected from the ratchet still gripped in my fist. "Okay, sir. I'm calm. We're all calm. We just have a misunderstanding here. I'm sure we can talk this out." I said. A hostage negotiator I am not.

He looked at his friend, muttering in Spanish, something about being shamed by a *gringa*. Looked in the car and spotted the brick of dope, eyes threatening to pop out of their sockets. He looked back at me and I could see his Scared circuit switch over to Panic. He had no clue how to handle this situation. Not that I had much room to talk, but this guy did things like this for a living. His How To Be A Miami Vice Villian book should have explained this scenario to him.

Stupid How-To books.

The shot-caller must be the peach pasteled turd sleeping on my shop floor. This day just keeps getting better.

"Whoever installed that, uh, stuff there damaged some wires to the ECU. I was only doing my job." Wasn't my damn fault. You jackasses should hire better mechanics.

Mexicans are legendary upholstery experts. How could an entire cartel of them allow Hillary to fabricate this seat? I kept that to myself and looked around the shop real quick. Not really surprised that no one had noticed the situation. Bobby was sanding an old primer gray Chevelle, bobbing his head and humming along to a Temptations song jamming from the car's radio. Ace and Nolan were chatting about the machine they tinkered on. Getting grease on his damn clothes. No one else had made it to work yet, thankfully.

Perfect time to stop being stupid and make a plan. "So what's the plan?" I asked Turquoise Pastel, hoping he could think of a less violent idea than the one I held in my fist. He looked as stupid and inconclusive as I did, so I stepped closer to him.

If I can get him in punching range...

"Is the car fixed?" he said, waving the gun at the GTO.

"I-I don't know. I just found the problem. The seat was smashing the wires. It might work now."

"Put the seat back. We are leaving."

Sounded great to me. I moved to do as he said, then hesitated when I heard the footsteps. A child's footsteps.

My heart froze. I gasped, forgetting to breathe.

"Clarice!" Nolan shouted, running over to me. He saw my look and must have thought I meant to scold him. He slowed and walked. "Dad showed me how to replace a faulty wire. See?" He held up a deformed wire like a trophy.

I smiled, inwardly cringing because my worst fear was happening. My son was merely feet away from a dangerous man with a gun. With a big grease stain on his uniform, dammit. I inched closer to my target, chin, throat, abdomen, groin, knees. My heart started beating again. My breathing resumed. "Nolan, honey. I'll look at that later. Right now I have to take care of this customer."

"Why does that man have a gun?" he asked, pointing at the weapon with perfect innocence. "Can I hold it? I had one just like it on *Metal Gear*."

Oh, goddamn.

"All right, *niño*. Get close to the *senora* there," Turquoise said, starting to panic again. Nolan just looked at him, completely unaware of what was happening. "I said GET OVER NEXT TO HER!" he shouted, waving the gun at my son and taking twenty years off my life span. When Nolan still didn't move, only stared, confused, Turquoise took a step towards him and pointed the gun at his head.

The weight of the tool in my hand should have been a cold weight. But it burned. Like an iron. Like an explosive that was a millisecond from going BOOM.

As soon as the Enemy moved in my son's direction, I sprang off my back foot with all my weight thrown behind a right-hand, extending it to a spot on the other side of his head. It hit the side of his neck with tremendous force, a gruesome crunch. I followed with a left-hook that smacked into his cheek, feeling like a slap after that crunching lead punch. The target crashed over the hood of the GTO, denting the metal panels with loud impacts, flailing his arms and the gun with no equilibrium.

Bobby appeared out of nowhere and swung a telephone pole arm down on Turquoise's gun hand, smashing his wrist against a fender, knocking the pistol to the floor. It clattered on the concrete like a heavy tool. Bobby grabbed him in a bear hug, roaring angrily with the squeezing effort as the man groaned out a painful breath. Stepping up to the giant and his catch, I snatched the pistol from Turquoise's belt. Bobby roared and squeezed again. The guy barked out another painful breath and lost consciousness.

Without meaning to, I mimicked his tortured noise. That was painful to watch.

"Nolan, go into the parlor!" Ace yelled, running up and grabbing the other revolver off the floor. Heavy footsteps pounded in the shop and he whipped the gun towards the open bays.

"Get the fuck on the ground!"

"On the floor, now! All of you!"

"Get down now, motherfucker!"

"Drop the guns, now! Put the guns down!"

Two cops came rushing in, guns drawn, screaming at the top of their lungs. I dropped the gun. So did Ace. We put our hands up but didn't get on the ground. We weren't the bad guys here.

"I said on the fucking ground! NOW." Some huge red-faced dude grabbed Ace and threw him on the concrete. Then he grabbed Bobby and, well, that was as far as he got. He tried his best to shove Bobby down, but the Custom Ace painting specialist just scowled at him. I almost laughed. The other cop, a Mexican guy with a look as nervous as the Pastel Brothers had, pointed his gun at me and motioned to the floor. I got down. I watched 20/20. Scared people with guns will kill you.

"Bobby, just get down, man. They'll figure it out," I told the big lug, almost laughing again. He got on the floor reluctantly, glaring at the policemen and their misdirected authority.

"Hands behind your motherfucking back. I said now!" the big cop yelled, pinning Bobby's arms, cuffing his wrists.

"Hey, asshole. You need to be handcuffing those guys,

not us," I argued.

"Shut up. Shut up! Just shut the fuck up, lady! I know how to do my job," the fat bastard shouted at me. He coughed several times, looking around, deciding what to do next. I was tempted to get up and crack him with the air ratchet. I looked at it. Couldn't believe it was still in my hand after that last blow. My knuckles bled freely, cut deeply, making the palm of my hand wet and sticky. I looked at my knockout victims. Both were sprawled in odd positions, looking like crash test dummies that had been thrown through windshields. The bruises on their jaws were already dark purple and swollen, split, leaking blood.

An intense feeling of pride welled up in me, making my eyes water, stretching a tight smile, throbbing to the beat of my split knuckle. I had protected my tribe.

And it throbbed so good.

But my proud disposition was short-lived. I began to get a bad vibe from the police continuing to treat us as the criminals and the Pastel Brothers as the victims. Pride devolved to fear, consolidating with words from the asshole cop with the ugly asthma face.

"You're under arrest. Give me your arms. Hold still!" he shouted at Ace, pinning him down with a knee between his shoulders, pressing his cheek into the concrete floor, distorting his face. Ace huffed with indignation, with pain at the four-hundred pound knee-log pushed into his vertebrae, popping them with dangerous flexing.

His hands were cuffed. He was jerked up. I found myself jerked up simultaneously. By instinct. Reaction to outrage. My man would not be treated this way. How dare he? How dare he think he can come in my house and touch one of mine like that?

HOW DARE HE.

I bounded towards the huge sonofabitch with rage thrashing in the depths of every muscle. Powering hard off the balls of my feet, I zipped at my new target with unnatural speed, fueled by anger so intense my vision literally turned red, and my hearing could only sense a high-pitched fizzling. The lit fuse on the Vendetta Cannon that boomed from my shoulders with a bestial snarl, thrown with all the explosive anger I could muster.

The cop turned his eyes to me as soon as I sprang, flinching, reflex from the startling movement in his peripheral. I was too far away and he had time to snap his head to the side right as my punch hit, neutralizing half its power as it plowed into his ear, ratchet scraping up his scalp, hair. Forward momentum rammed my chest into his side, an immovable wall that promptly knocked the wind from me on impact.

"Oof!" I sputtered. This was probably a little out of my weight class. I went for it anyway, vision deepening with red fuel, high-pitched fizzle threatening to blow my eardrums, the fight junkie out of her cage and swinging as hard and as fast as she could, arms blurring with knockout power in either fist. My target swung his gun towards me, caught a few punches on his face, arms, stumbled, dropped his gun arm to crank it through the air a few rotations to gain balance. I dropped the ratchet so I could throw faster and pounced on him again, five-punch combination that only brushed his face as he fell backwards, not quite fast enough to beat the pull of gravity on a huge falling body.

Dammit!

He hit the floor with a wallop, keys clanging on concrete, gun belt and vest creaking, elbows and boots thumping. "You stupid cunt!" he coughed out, wheezing, face scarlet. "I got something for you."

I had a moment to realize I should have jumped on top of him. I wasn't in a ring with boxing rules. He unsnapped a large cylindrical compartment on his belt and removed a can of pepper spray. He drew it with a well-practiced fluidity and sprayed the motherfucker right in my eyes, covering my entire head and upper body with incapacitating chemicals.

"Gaah! You prick," I spat. Then sneezed. Sneezed again. My eye muscles locked up, squinting my eyes hard enough to give me thirty years of wear on my Butterface. Eyebrows pushing down. Forehead flexing. Mouth puckered, throat sucked in, a vacuum attempting to pump some air through an esophagus I knew was uncontrollably inflamed and constricted. Every little breath sucked in more pepper particles, circulating them deep into my lungs and further arresting my respiratory system. No air, no muscle power. The Mexican cop finally decided to assist his partner and had me on my face within seconds, hands cuffed painfully behind my back. My oxygen-deprived brain could only wonder at the trained ease the officer had shown in trussing me like a rodeo animal.

"Clarice!" Ace yelled. Dust and Oil Dry stuck to his lips that were pressed to the concrete once again.

"What?" I croaked. Gasp air, resist the choke, gasp air, resist the choke. SNEEZE!

Shit. This stuff handed my butt to me. My first TKO. But a TKO is not a KO...

"You okay?"

"Great...Never...Better," I wheezed, snot running out of my nose like water. Gasp air, resist the choke...

"Shut up, shut up!" the Nazi cop shouted. It took him a year-and-a-half to get up. He coughed several times, looking back and forth between me and Ace, angry, confused. He coughed again. "You!" He pointed at me. "Are under arrest for assault on a police officer." He looked over at Ace, at me again, determining that we were securely detained for the time being. He walked over to Bobby, moving stiffly on legs that weren't used to so much excitement, squatted down and stared at his face. Holstered his gun, but kept the pepper spray handy. He frowned at Bobby, trying to get an impression of how he would fit into the situation. The cop shook his head, coming to some kind of decision, stood and walked over to the Pontiac. Stuck his head in the open driver's side. Glanced around and spotted the drugs and cut-open seat. He nodded and grunted, limped over to stand between my husband and me again. He said, "You are under arrest for possession of narcotics."

"You got me fucked up, fat boy!" Bobby exploded.

"You're making a huge mistake," Ace sputtered from dusty lips.

"Gonna...Kick...Your...Big ass." Gasp air, resist choke...

"Shut up, shut up! THE LAW IS WHAT I SAY IT IS!" he continued, yelling over our protests. "And, you're under arrest for conspiracy to traffic narcotics."

"You got me fucked up!" Bobby cursed, rolling over to try and stand. The pepper spray was aimed at him and he quit.

"Not you, nigger! These two! THESE TWO! Shut your stupid black hole before I charge you too. Shut up!"

"Soon as... I get... my breath," I gasped, squinting through one barely opened eye to focus on my target, chin, throat, abdomen, groin, knees, completely ignoring his fraudulent arrest in my mission to stop him. I gained my feet, he noticed my intent and ruthlessly dosed me with another burst of chemicals, dropping me to the floor and foiling my plans.

My face locked up again, squinting so hard my eyes felt like hot irons being driven into my head. My diaphragm froze as if I had been nailed with a solid body punch, inflamed nerves cut off from communication pulses that tell my lungs to breath. BREATHE, CLARICE!

The tiny gasp I finally sucked in turned into a sneeze, ejecting the precious air before my lungs had a chance to utilize it. This was undoubtedly the most inconvenient feeling I've experienced. The motherfucking cop had TKO in a can. I was immobilized and completely helpless. And humiliated to boot.

And suddenly very frightened.

This couldn't be happening. I had saved my people, taken out the Bad Guys that had threatened our well being. The cops were supposed to be on our side, dragging these criminals off my shop floor and congratulating us for calling the police and overcoming the perps.

My fear grew, fumed in my near-unconscious daze, blooming with cold fire that spread down my arms and legs, up my spine and neck, steamed from my ears in a renewed fizzle, lighting another fuse. My eyes cracked open, blurry, red, pried open by a will that didn't know the meaning of surrender, having every intention of slaughtering the pig that had so quickly turned our big win into a nightmarish setback.

I wanted a taste of those pork chops big boy was holding.

My fists flexed and trembled, willing to work without oxygen, engines that continued to run hard even when starved of fuel. But they were cuffed, rendered obsolete. My legs were not much better. Free, but practically useless, flaccid of all but slight tremors. Willing to kick, but unable to. No matter. I only needed them to hold me up for a few seconds.

My Enemy pointed the pepper spray at Bobby, at Ace, daring them to give him an excuse. "Anybody else? Keep your mouths shut or I'll shut 'em for you. Like I said." He coughed, looked at his partner. "Hector, call it in. And check the ETA of our assistance."

"Okay, Jimmy," Hector said, nodding. He turned his back to us and spoke codes into his walkie-talkie. The air-compressor turned off, its rapid thump-pump petering out, stopping completely, hissing a release of pressure that was built up in the hoses. The shop became silent except for my wheezing gasps and Pork Chop cop's coughing fits.

Engines raced outside the shop. With surreal detachment, I amazed myself by taking a second to admire the exhaust notes of what I knew were 4.6 liter Interceptor engines. Crown Victoria police cars. Hopefully carrying cops with common sense.

Footsteps and voices sounded from the front of the building, talking, questioning loudly, moving through my parlor with rude disregard. Two men in uniforms rushed in through the hallway door, slowing and relaxing as they took in the scene and deemed it secure. Three more officers popped in through an open garage bay, ducking around a car lift to walk toward us quickly while searching the rest of the shop for activity. They crouch-walked, guns and heads whipping around with no wasted movement. A single policeman ducked in through the rear bay door, completing their grid of the building. Security sweep 101.

"What's the status?" asked one of the new arrivals, a muscle-bound ego on legs, with a buzz cut and sunglasses that came from the same cookie cutter as the rest of his pals.

Pork Chop answered, "We came in and found the perps holding the victims at gunpoint. We disarmed them, determined they were conspiring to traffic drugs with this white car here," he said, pointing at the GTO.

My legs straightened like hydraulic cylinders, standing me up, speechless. Ace and Bobby found their voices, however.

"YOU'RE THE PERPS!" Bobby bellowed, voice booming off the steel walls with startling effect. Everyone cringed and looked at him. Ace flopped around trying to get his feet under him, outraged, fuming protest from dusty lips.

"Possession of narcotics, assault on a police officer, aggravated assault on both of the victims here," Pork Chop said, counting off on his sausage fingers. The officers nodded, one of them patting Pork Chop on the back. Several thumbs-up directed at Hector.

I started in my Enemy's direction, just sort of stumbled on numb legs with the same detached, oxygen-deprived thoughts that had noted the engine exhaust tones, staring at a big red face that I wanted to hurt, to make it stop talking, stop lying, stop hurting my family's future with every jounce and jiggle of its jowls. I noted an angle, a bull's eye on my target that would accomplish my goal, stop the bastard that had instigated a stunning catastrophe.

Ooh, come and give momma a taste of those pork chops.

I stumbled, unnoticed by the collaborating police, over to ol' Jiggle Jowls, devoid of emotion, focused only on the intent, angling toward the bull's eye that would surely make this nightmare cease once I hit it.

I stopped in front of my target. Looked up at my bull's eye with lust. I noted, like a hawk dispassionately eyeing a lesser bird, that my bull's eye was still flapping away, huffing emphysemic fabrications about what had taken place here.

I looked at Hector, the only officer there that didn't look like he was enjoying a hard-on from arresting innocent people. "I was the one that called you guys," I wheezed at him, then I gripped my handcuff chain and lunged forward with a head butt aimed at his partner. The crown of my head rammed into Pork Chop's chin, arcing up to smash his lips against his teeth and bust his nose, warm blood spraying down my face, into my eyes. He gave a monstrous grunt as the pain and shock from the blow set in, astounding him, setting off a chain of coughs that made me think I had hit his pepper spray somehow, spraying him with a nice dose. His pals rushed me. Pork Chop fumbled at his belt, roaring with fury, up came the spray again, hosing me and the three that had grabbed my legs and shoulders and tackled me to the ground in a cloud of no-breath. I had a moment to realize the chemicals in my hair are what had caused Pork

Chop's coughing attack, and would probably cause him to die a slow, painful asthmatic death.

Yay, no-breathe!

Wish I could head butt him again.

The shop floor rudely contorted my face, smelling strongly of oil. Ten feet away Ace was still flopping around. Bobby was cheering for me to hit him again. The officers yelled over each other trying to establish procedure, coughing, squinting angry eyes.

The last thing I heard before the no-breathe KOed me was my own impartial thoughts wondering who would get the grease stains out of Nolan's uniform.

PART VII

Central Mississippi Correctional Facility
October 10, 2011

"CARTER! CLARICE CARTER! Visitation," the officer announced. She stood in front of a stainless steel picnic table flipping through a count roster, a list of inmate's names, numbers, and bed assignments attached to a clipboard. Her blue uniform top labeled her as a CO 1, her thin ponytail and short fingernails labeled her as a black woman on a budget.

She smiled as I approached, and I reminded myself that she was usually a nice black woman on a budget, a person I should at least attempt to be cordial to. One of the few officers I've met that wasn't a power-tripping retard. Unfortunately for the friendly COs like her, the situation that landed me in this dump has made me, let's call it, "sensitive," to police authority in any form.

Several of the power abusers were on the receiving end of some very eloquent threats, and a few thrashing haymakers, from a former pro fighter now known as offender J1332. One extremely unfortunate lady caught a left-hook to her muffin top after pepper spraying me, twice, (which I seem to have developed an immunity to) and another large and lovely lady ran head first into a wall after I fought loose from a group of COs attempting to hold me and turned my fury in her direction. She wanted to press charges, but abruptly ended her hissy fit after I pointed out that a jury wouldn't convict a cinder block wall.

I've been sprayed and locked down five times already. I simply can't stand people telling me what I can and can't do.

An almost exact repeat of what happened when they first locked me up in the county jail. I have twenty bosses, and the higher they rank, the higher they rate on the Idiot Scale.

And I just got here. For Christ's sake, people. Grumbling, I walked away from another source of strife, a group of women I had no wish to be around, but was forced to live with. They watched soap operas on a small TV mounted high up on a wall. Around thirty black women and a few whites, one Latina, lounged around picnic tables, plopped in plastic chairs or sat on the floor bundled up in blankets or thermals, oblivious to anything outside of this little world. Truly products of their environment, they were broken long ago to submit and accept these conditions as their home and life. Some were serving life. And instead of hitting up the law library every week looking for a loophole in the system, they were yucking it up at the card tables or staring at eye candy on the idiot box.

Incarceration, I've found, is a serious education in human behavior. It is simply amazing what a person can adapt to. And confounding. And scary.

And it pissed me off.

I shook my head in renewed anger, struggling to refocus it so I wouldn't start bitching about all there is to be mad about around here. I stopped in front of the CO I planned on being nice to, and even planted a big fake smile on my face to challenge my will. It was probably a wretched mug, like you'd see on Mrs. Potato Head.

"Hello, Officer Pruet," Mrs. Potato Head said.

"Hello, Offender J1332."

"Any idea who is here to see me?"

"Your attorney."

"Great. I've been working on a new lawyer joke to tell his sorry ass," I said, losing the smile. The women behind me ah-ed together at something on the television. Damn whiny soaps.

"Oh, come on now. He might have some good news for you this time."

"Uh-huh. Like the truth? As in, I'm innocent and get to go home?"

She smiled, raised her eyebrows with skepticism. "They're all innocent," she sighed, rolling her eyes. Made me want to slug her. "Let's go, now. You ready?"

"Sure," I replied, thinking about doing ninety days in lock down for assaulting her. Deciding against it, barely, I refreshed my cordial Mrs. Potato Head and grinned and beared it. Attempting to regain our positive rapport, I said, "Got my mani-pedi, boss tan, Karen Millen dress and Gucci heels. How's my hundred dollar hairdo look?" I said, posing and patting my hair like it was styled and shining like diamonds. It was in a short, ugly ponytail just like hers.

She laughed. "Looks fine to me. Have ya taken your medication today?" She pointed at my prisoner's uniform of black and white striped pants and white pullover with MDOC CONVICT heat-stamped on the back. "Looks more like Barker than Millen, honey. Even Halle Berry would look rough in that."

That brought a small smile. Bob Barker made everything from toothbrushes to mattresses for prisons worldwide. Mistaking the Price Is Right geezer for a fashion designer would certainly make me eligible for anti-psychotic meds. My smile widened. "No biggie. I'll rock my Barker getup. And anyways, if I go too feminine I start to look like a transsexual."

Officer Pruet snickered, pinching her wide nose. Eyes glittering with humor, she shook her head at me and turned to walk toward the zone's main entrance. I followed, glancing left, right, at the empty beds, wondering what time it was. Most of the women here could tell you the time according to what soap opera was on. I was determined to never become so institutionalized or media programmed, so I asked the screw.

Pruet looked behind us at the TV, then gave me a look like I couldn't have asked a more stupid question. "It's one o'clock. General Hospital just came on."

I nearly reeled from her answer. She was doing hard time like us!

"You late for an appointment?" she continued with inane sarcasm.

"Nah, nothing special," I said, gritting my teeth.

Just late for the Big Show, lady. That's all. The mega event of knocking the dusty grills out of all the smart mouth COs like you. REAL late for that. Perhaps we'll reschedule.

She kept glancing at me, an uneasy expression forming as she noticed my feral grin suddenly bloom and hint that I just might have a special appointment after all.

The grin had to be ugly, scary, Mrs. Evil Potato Head. But I kept it there.

It felt good.

The concrete building was L-shaped and divided in two sections, A-zone and B-zone, with fifteen-foot tall circular guard towers in the center of each zone. The tower windows were square, covered in steel grates, and gave the tower officer a panoramic view of the zone, cubicles, and showers. The concrete floor was painted a soft psych ward blue, chipped, scraped, faded and stained with everything from orange pepper spray, blood, to homemade black and yellow hair dye. A low cinder block wall, maybe four-feet high, sectioned off cubicles not unlike an office building. Instead of desks and computers, the cubicles encompassed two steel bunk beds, black, with green foam mattresses, white sheets and pillowcases, locker boxes, and four female convicts with all their collective drama.

The concrete walls were odd white tones of the lowest quality pigments. Like someone put a spoonful of mustard in a jar of mayonnaise and slathered it all over everything, uneven, thick and thin, with too much mustard in the mix here and there. The lack of quality control made my obsessive-compulsive axe really grind. Like fingernails digging into a chalkboard so hard it flashed sparks and little wisps of foul smoke. Those of us that were intelligently aware of our surroundings, and understood what it all meant relative to the rest of the world, lived in a perpetual state of cringing pooh-pooh face.

A Thorazine patient stumbled by. Uncoordinated, pants so dirty the white stripes looked black. Natty, filthy hair and unhealthy skin. She was white, though had evidently tallied up enough days away from the shower to make her look Hispanic. But she was so content, so damn gleeful, dancing around in her own little world. Planet Happiness, with bright sunshine and friendly, cuddly moons of Everything is Funny and I Love Laughing-Drooling-Snotty Expressions orbiting around her silly smile. If I stayed here much longer, I would start to envy her. Though I'm sure I would never take the ultimate step like she did, give up hope for a super tranquilized life of unawareness.

"Ignorance is bliss," I murmured.

Pruet followed my eyes over to the woman joyously doing the Thorazine Shuffle, giggling, clapping, twirling. "I guess it really can be," she agreed.

The zone's main entrance was next to the tower. We stopped in front of it and Pruet keyed her walkie-talkie. "B-zone tower, open thirty-five," she said, releasing the button and looking up at the tower window. The tower CO stepped to the window, waved, turned a knob on the control board. The heavy steel lock buzzed, clicked, the white door whined open on its dry scraping track. We walked through into a long hallway with more psych ward blues and mustard whites. The chemical scent of industrial floor wax burned my nose. A slim black lady in prison stripes was wrestling with a floor-buffing machine behind us as we walked toward the administration section of the unit. Officer Pruet followed behind me as security protocol mandated, watching to see if I picked up or passed any contraband. I was a good girl and managed not to pass any shanks or pick up any drugs.

We arrived at the A-zone tower and turned to go through the main exit. Pruet did her thing on the radio again, advising the tower to open the twin gates in front of the door. We walked outside.

The October afternoon sky was gorgeous. Deep blue with fluffs and puffs of the cutest clouds, mostly high-altitude cirrus with random jet vapor trails shot through. Reminded me of one of Nolan's first paintings, making me smile.

The grandiose sky scene was ruined by the rotten tooth below it. Concrete buildings of the most despicable design sprawled desecration across the acres, each sectioned off with twin razor wire-topped fences, their variety of energies mixing and clashing to form an unpredictable economy.

Most of the quiet, frightened women had been shipped to the ape warehouse just because our capricious government figured out a way to make a buck on it.

Women afraid of everything in here and deteriorating on a sharp curve, confined to the lower rungs of the ladder where the hustled and the punked cling to existence.

The core members of the mix were more emotionally complex, more active in the range between inferior and superior and not likely to stay status quo for very long.

And then there were the very strong women. The Alphas. Some were respected for not using their abilities to take advantage of others. Most instigated cruelty and physical abuse to anyone they perceived as marks, inmates and officers alike.

Trapped. Scared. Feared. Animals vying for status.

I turned left onto a concrete walkway with a corrugated steel roof that blocked the sun, cooling the air and casting a rectangular shadow on the freshly cut grass. Grasshoppers and gnats swarmed over the green clippings. The administration building was the same ugly formed-concrete structure as the other buildings, but with more dimensions, more doors for a cafeteria, barbershop, watch commander's office, and other penitentiary facilities.

As we approached the visitation section, a strong breeze blew through the walkway, scattering stray grass blades over my cheap white shoes, dislodging strands from my hair tie. A huge cumulus cloud moved overhead, hiding the sun, making the gushing wind chilly. As I finger combed my hair, I heard echoes of barking and smelled the stink of wet dogs, bloodhounds that were kept in kennels close by, at the Emergency Response Team headquarters. Those jerks were the worst power trippers. ERT loved to intimidate and assault prisoners, even more than the inmate bullies. Stripping a girl naked and tearing up her property in front of eighty of her peers was just a warm-up for them. Open your mouth to protest the degrading of your fellow convict and they'll strip you naked and tear up your property for your compassion. Ask me how I know. By then they'll be high on power lust and want another hit. The zone or the entire building could potentially get shook down, and ERT will rock their jollies from finding miscellaneous drugs and weapons and roughing up disgruntled women that fight like men.

They were freaking terrorists. Full of threats like the one that gave me chill bumps now, barking dogs illustrating a scene with an escaped convict being torn apart by the pack.

I scowled and tried to shake it out of my mind. But the image continued, premonitory, expanding on the idea of escape with me as the star of the stunt. It felt possible, all of a sudden. It felt like it was meant to be. I gasped as a jolt of anxious adrenaline flooded my arms and legs, priming my body to hold up for the mad adventure circulating in my mind.

I paused and glanced at Officer Pruet, with what I knew was an odd, guilty look.

Stupid. As if she could hear me thinking about escape. She couldn't, and kept walking.

Deciding those thoughts were too high-risk while in the presence of the blue shirts, I made a mental note to consider the subject again later. Then focused on the door to the front and the hypocritical lawyer waiting to stick a fork in me.

The door, labeled "Visitation," buzzed and we walked through into a small room with white tiles and mustard walls, stopped in front of a small metal desk. A CO sat behind it, an obese black lady of middle age squeezed into a padded chair that was visibly flexing under her bulk. A beehive-shaped weave on her head reflected the light, a shiny cone with a chubby face at its base that held an oily sheen of its own. Her name badge said her name was Loquesha Howard, but that sounded too long and complex for this lady. She looked at me and I thought her name badge should say Thud or Oof. A box of Popeye's fried chicken perched on the edge of the desk and filled the room with its secret spicy grease. A door with a Plexiglas window was to my left. I looked through it, into the visitation room, where I spotted my lawyer sitting at a table with a briefcase on it.

"I'll be back in an hour," Officer Pruet told me, signing a log on the desk.

"I thought attorney visits were longer," I said, frowning.

"They are. But they rarely last longer than it takes to deliver the bad news."

I scowled at her, reevaluating my opinion of this silly screw. She may not abuse her authority, but that didn't necessarily mean she was nice or smart. In fact, Pruet had to be one STUPID fucking broad to think she could keep talking to me like that. I made a serious effort to unclench my fists, which couldn't wait for the next stupid thing to come out of her mouth. Turned and walked to the visitation room door. The CO struggled up from her chair, which gave a squeak and groan I swear sounded like relief, and waddled over to me, fumbling with a large ring of keys attached to her belt. She selected a key, unlocked the door, tumblers clicking loudly. She apparently wasn't aware of her girth because I had to suck in a breath to shimmy past her, cringing as she wheezed her laborious chicken breath in my face. She locked the door behind me.

My attorney stood up from a green plastic chair behind a long wooden table, a white dude in his late fifties, grayish hair, smooth shaved face with a bulbous, red alcoholic's nose and flushed cheeks. His gray eyes would probably look a really pretty blue after a trip to the Betty Ford Clinic and several shots of vitamin B12. His brown suit was expensive but very unclean, rumpled, like he had just pulled it from the trunk of his car and hurriedly dressed in the parking lot before coming inside.

"You look like a stool sample," I greeted the man, sitting down in a chair opposite from him. Rested my arms on the table.

"Ah-ha," he chortled. "No lawyer jokes this time?" He sat down.

"That was my lawyer joke. You officers of the court are a bunch of damn sewer surfers. Like evil Ninja Turtles in dookie colored suits."

"Ah, good to see you still have your sense of humor, Clarice." He opened the small black briefcase on the table in front of him. The latch snapped, echoing in the quiet room. I glanced up at the drop ceiling, around at the other tables and chairs, while he rifled through some papers, jerky movements that showed he had no specific item he was searching for. A make-work tic that all lawyers seemed to do. Hey, they have to at least look like they are earning your money, right?

"So. What's the good news? You work up any connections in the Court of Appeals?" I inquired.

"Ah, no. I don't think a judge of that caliber would take a chance on overturning your case."

"Meaning what?"

"Meaning, ah, that there are numerous cases in the system that an appeals judge would reverse before yours. Cases with far less incriminating evidence. A judge would take serious political and professional criticism from favoring your case without significant new evidence that would warrant a new trial."

"What incriminating evidence? My trial judge was an idiot. Surely the higher judges can see through all that bullshit, see that it was made up," I stormed, leaning forward and staring into his eyes.

He dropped his gaze first. "Ah, we've been over this before, Clarice. The, ah, trial was horrendous, a slam-dunk for the prosecution. Two arresting officers testified that you and your husband were found assaulting the victims. The testimony from a police officer holds serious weight in court."

"Wait a minute. Victims? Victims?! Do you think I'm guilty, too?" I said, voice rising to a shout.

The CO at the visitation desk stood up. My lawyer waved at her, signaling everything was okay. "Ah, sorry. I've been reading the Attorney General's response brief. The, ah, cartel men claimed they came to your shop to use the phone. They said you unfairly stereotyped them, assumed they were drug guys just because of the way they looked, and tried to employ them to drive the shipment of drugs to an unknown destination. When they refused, you allegedly tried physical persuasion, with your fighting expertise, that got out of hand."

"But I'm the one that called the motherfreaking cops!" I said for probably the thousandth time in the last year-and-a-half. I sighed, closed my eyes.

"I know," he said, making soothing gestures with his hands. "Prosecution said you called in an attempt to clean up your mess." He paused, pursed his lips. "Your fingerprints were on one of the bricks of cocaine. Theirs weren't. And both you and your husband's prints were on the guns. The car had untraceable license and VIN plates that prosecution claimed could have been easily attained through your automotive connections. And to put the icing on the cake, those cartel guys had spotless records." He grunted. "The evidence, however false, was overwhelmingly against you. My firm has studied your case from top to bottom for eighteen months now, and we can't see any new evidence that can be presented to the Court of Appeals or the Mississippi Supreme Court." He paused again, a dejected frown appearing to show me how sorry he was for taking my money for such a stick-in-my-ass result. His eyes watered a little, lawyerly showmanship kicking in to sell it, like a good final argument to a jury that's been unimpressed with his performance thus far.

"Shit."

"I'm truly sorry, Clarice. I, ah, have to recommend that you and your husband hire another firm, though for the life of me, I don't know what they could do to get you out of this. I'm sorry," he said again, dropping the papers back in the briefcase, ending the ruse.

"It's over, then," I breathed to myself, exhaling long and slow as a numbness enveloped me. Eyes wide, staring at nothing, I sensed but didn't see my attorney stand up and leave, a warm shadow tinged with high-quality vodka retreating silently to the far left of the room. A buzz of the

119

lock. Heavy click of a security door.

And all hope of freedom walking out with him.

After months of hassle with the feds, I had convinced them my home and businesses were bought legally, but failed to convince them about the property in the buildings, which they confiscated. I sold everything we had left to pay the firm to represent Ace and myself. They took all our money. I couldn't afford to hire more attorneys if I wanted to. I was sitting on absolute rock bottom. Broke. Busted. Disgusted.

My scalp suddenly hurt. I became aware of my hands gripping the sides of my hair, white knuckled fists squeezing, grasping it. I don't know why. Maybe just to make sure I could still feel something.

Feel something.

I gripped harder, pulling my hair tie loose and bunching big clumps of hair above my ears. Cheap shampoo offended my nose, Bob Barker crap that had the odor of dog shampoo and made me feel like a flea scratching degenerate for using it. My hands caught another gear and red-hot swords pierced my skull, yet I couldn't quite feel it. I was far beyond awareness of pain, fully desensitized to the scalpel of stress that carved my guts into ribbons and made the tears streaming down my face burn like acid, an auto-reply my body produced to show me it still knew how to do its job even though I had vacated the driver's seat.

My body was crying. My mind was down the rabbit hole.

My nose dripped onto the table, thick cloudy drops that splattered and darkened the wood. I stared at the puddle, feeling my diaphragm trying to expand to sniffle the mess from my nostrils and cease this indecent display. An involuntary snort filled my throat with warm, salty fluid that nearly choked me, forcing me to wake the hell up and swallow.

I searched for sensation other than the hot and wet no-crying and found none. There was nothing to sense, a desolate embodiment that was once mighty and bountiful, but was now torn and stripped from heart-wrenching losses, one right after another.

I recognized the despair threatening to consume me as being deeper and more profound than anything I've ever experienced, far worse than the loss I felt after retiring from fighting. My family, my husband and son, my home and businesses, friends, employees. People that depended on me to provide for their homes and families and friends. Lost. Gone.

Taken.

Everything was taken from me.

Somewhere deep inside of me a switch was suddenly flipped. A switch so heavy with life-changing consequences weighing it down that it required fight-or-flight instincts and immense psyche power to even budge it. It clicked so hard and so fast it felt like a giant had snapped a twig. Sensation approached, far in the distance, I could feel its heavy chugging towards me, a freight train a thousand miles long, heavy tonnage speeding on a track that just barely guided a massive, violent beast.

My hands gripped even harder, anticipating, spreading the pain from my scalp down my face like a red blanket, tinting my vision. My arms flushed, tingling with heat. My throat constricted with emotion, boiling rage that came to a head as the violent freight pulled in to station. My arms flexed, vascular and alien, the arms of a being ruled by instincts of dominant, physical action. A new driver was behind the wheel. One that knew violence like an old lover, knew how to mold it into many shapes and forms of hurt without regard to morals or mercy.

A driver that understood Clarice the Wife and Mother could never break the laws and soil her pretty pink fingernails with what must be done.

A driver that knew how to take.

I felt like people should be watching me do something, do something to some body. Cheering for pain infliction and blood and bodies slapping down on the mat.

Mat. Ring. Where's the ring?

I glanced around, expecting to see a roped off square with a beer logo and referee dancing and dodging while a spirited crowd shouted my name all around us.

My name.

My flushed arms lightened, my veins receded, and with it all feeling of doubt. A transformation had taken place, leaving me with many certitudes. The first and most obvious was I no longer felt alien. I was the alien. And confidence of the most supreme form had replaced the plague of fears. I felt the dried tears on my face and wondered how I could ever cry, how I could ever submit to such a superfluous, counter productive emotion. I was the Shocker.

I am the Shocker!

Having never experienced this persona outside of boxing relations, it took me a moment to accept what had become of me. But only a moment. I smiled.

Oh, yeah. This is just what I needed. Welcome back, baby. MWAH!

I hugged myself.

My homecoming was rudely interrupted by the door on the far side of the room buzzing and clicking again. It opened, a Latino gentleman entered like he owned the place. Middle-aged and of medium height and small build, he was well-groomed with salt and pepper hair combed to the side, smooth face with a black mustache and chin beard cropped short. Tasteful cream suit with darker toned patches on the elbows. Bow tie. He looked like a college professor. I stared at him. He stared back, dark eyes squinting and flickering to analyze my tear-stained face, bloodshot eyes and disarrayed hair, puddle on the table. Back to my face. My stressed appearance was in stark contrast with my relaxed, focused, and smiling expression.

The professor walked toward me exhibiting a swagger that told me he either wielded great power or had really big balls. He stopped on the other side of the table from me. Unbuttoned his jacket. Sat down in the chair my attorney had used. He continued to stare into my eyes. Through my eyes. Like a damn soul gaze.

"You are not Clarice Carter," he said in a pleasant, lecturing tone without accent. I remained silent, smiling, relaxed. Confident. Patient and unconcerned. He looked at the puddle of tears and snot again, pursed his lips. "You are Clarice Ares. The Shocker. Now. Again."

Whoa. This dude really did gaze into my soul. My expression didn't change, however.

"That is correct. Recently reconciled." I hugged myself, then waved a hand in his direction. Kudos. "I admire your insight."

"It is what I do."

"And what is that?"

He didn't answer, just squinted and analyzed. I guess I should've wondered who he was and how he got in here to see me without being on the approved visitation list. Clarice would have fretted about that, I suppose, but not me. Maybe later.

Who gives a shit? I laughed.

He stared for a moment more, then said, "My name is Ignacio. Your predicament regarding the appeal recently came to my attention and I wish to help you."

"Really."

"Sincerely, yes."

"How is it that you know the Shocker? You a boxing fan?"

"Indirectly, yes. I run a corporation that owns many

smaller businesses, some with charities that fund even smaller establishments. One in particular is a quaint little boxing gym in Juarez that had the pleasure of producing two world champions. You destroyed one of them in your final fight at the Blue Horizon." He paused and gave an amused smile. "I lost a considerable sum of money."

"You bet on the wrong horse."

"Admittedly, I knew that before placing the wager."

"You knowingly bet on a loser?"

"She was no loser, and I am nothing if not loyal to my people," he said, deadpan serious.

I smiled. "Consuela Torres. How is she?"

"Not good. She was never the same after you knocked her out. She fought three more times, lost twice, then retired. Senora Torres now works at one of my garment factories. A manager, I believe."

"Damn. You rarely hear a happy ending to a boxer's life."

"*Es verdad*," that's the truth, he replied.

"I mean, they usually end up broke, OD'ed on drugs, or in prison. Like me." A menacing look flashed over my face. A solar flare erupting from a riled sun. Teeth gnashing, I said in a clipped voice, "Even though I'm innocent."

"I know you are innocent," he said quietly, without hesitation, looking me in the eye.

I sat up. "Really."

"Sincerely, yes."

We engaged in another stare down. "Great power and big balls," I murmured.

"Pardon me?" He raised his eyebrows.

"What do you want?"

He laid his hands flat on the table, thick gold rings over perfectly manicured nails. They gleamed with clear polish.

"Truthfully, I wish to ease my conscience. To aid you in some way, perhaps influence the locals so you can live comfortably in here."

"And you have that kind of influence?"

"I do."

"Know anybody in the Court of Appeals?"

"Regretfully, no."

"Then you can't help me."

Silence again. The fluorescent lights overhead hummed. A door buzzed-clicked behind me. I turned to look and saw an older lady in green and white stripes, a trustee, through the Plexiglas that I recognized as a high-ranking Latin Queen. The trustee had a mop in her hand, the head of it in a bucket of soapy water that rolled as she pushed it into an adjoining room with snack and soda machines. The lady glanced at me, did a double take and stared at Ignacio. She gasped, put a latex gloved hand to her mouth. In the silence we heard her say, "El Maestro."

The Teacher. Hmm. I looked back at my visitor, menace flashing again. I've read about this guy. "I don't mean to be presumptuous, but a Mexican business owner, one that runs a 'corporation', usually translates into laymen's English as a cartel kingpin."

"I cannot refute that," he said amiably. "However-"

"Scum of the earth," I growled.

He gave a shocked expression, one he wasn't used to displaying. Eyes big, mouth a perfect O. It slowly turned into a scowl, dark and ominous, displeasure at having been goosed into showing unstrategic emotion.

"And you want to ease your conscience, as you say, because those drugs and those two Nash Bridges thugs that came into my shop were yours."

"Again, regretfully this time, I cannot refute that."

"And those asshole pigs that ruined my fucking family's life were on your payroll, as well." My solar glare looked like it was burning his face. I whispered to him, lips quivering, "I was just collateral damage to you, right?"

He flinched, slowly regained his composure, but

remained silent.

"I'll take your silence as assent. Tell you what, you dirt bag. I would like to make it through the rest of today without murdering a sonofabitch like you with my bare hands." My fists flexed hard, started shaking in anticipation. The Teacher put a hand to his waist. "If you don't leave right now. I. Will. Kill. You." I said, enunciating each word with a snarl.

The Teacher held up a hand as if asking for a moment of consideration. With the other hand, he pulled aside his jacket and showed me a giant gun in a shoulder holster. I couldn't believe my eyes. In prison.

Great power and big balls, no shit.

He said, "I wasn't worried about Mrs. Carter. But I expected nothing less from the Shocker." Closing his jacket, he stood. "My people and I respect you greatly. We will continue pursuing avenues to aid your release. And, for what it is worth, I am deeply sorry, Senora Shocker."

Sorry?

I sprang up, knocking my chair several feet behind me in a loud clatter of plastic on tiles. The Teacher was slower, jumping backwards, almost tripping over his chair, hopping around to get balanced. He stepped around the chair, eyes on me, backed away quickly, unholstering the gun. The Latin Queen in the snack room burst into a stream of desperate sounding Spanish.

"That gun doesn't scare me, El Maestro. Leave before my fists taste your blood." I was panting, nearly foaming at the mouth in my desire to attack this man.

He nodded, gave me a look of sadness and regret before bravely turning his back and holstering the weapon. Swaggered over to the door. It buzzed, clicked, closed behind him with a heavy finality.

I turned around to see the Latin Queen looking at me like I was Satan incarnate, still muttering rapid-fire Spanish in what sounded like prayer.

The CO at the visitation desk was standing, bent over the box of Popeye's, wide butt jacked up and looking like the rear tires on a dune buggy. I walked to the door and motioned for her to open it. She looked at my Power Puff Girl hair, feral grin, blood red eyes and veins standing up from my fists. Back to my grin. Her eyes widened, mouth opened.

She shook her head no.

PART VIII

Juarez, Chihuahua
Mexico
October 11, 2011

THE DARK BLUE Gulfstream IV shot out of the bank of clouds above the Rio Grande at over 300mph, streamlined aerodynamics and precise navigation performing a turbulence-free flight. Small red lights on the wings blinked at intervals. The down-flaps shifted slightly, angling the aircraft on a descent that broke up more ranks of clouds, most bright and fluffy white, some dark and thickening with ice, dust, and precipitation. Tempests in infancy.

The ground appeared a few blinks later, terra firma that looked especially sharp after hours of immersion in the fluffy canopy of potential thunderheads. Beams of sunlight filtered down in rays that faded but still brightened the greens and browns of small dry climate shrubs and cacti peppering the desert as far as the eye could see. The sun hid behind a mass of blinding whiteout to the left of the southbound jet, nearing its peak and alerting the agenda conscious that it was time to prepare for the noontime siesta.

El Maestro sat in a roomy recliner next to the first window facing the sun, the only passenger on board. An irritable expression seemed permanently stained on his face. But the mood didn't keep him from gazing out the window and appreciating the aesthetics of the sky and land surrounding his desert home.

The jet banked slightly to the west. What appeared to be a small airport came into view. As the pilot maneuvered closer, the vague airport became a large estate with a private

129

airstrip. A huge villa with a brown tiled roof commanded the center stage, with a smaller structure of similar build off to one side. Several acres around the buildings and runway were fenced in, thick red brick columns with steel poles in a pleasing octagon, with smaller fences inside corralling horses, chickens, pigs, and burros. Large steel roofed sheds stood next to the corrals.

Men, and a few robust women, were on horseback or riding ATVs, going about their tasks like busy ants, herding the animals and hauling loads of various ranching by-products.

The pilot circled the area and lined up with the runway, descending smoothly. Seconds later, a muffled chirp of tires and compression of struts could be heard in the cabin where El Maestro was calmly unbuckling his seat harness. The plane taxied toward a large hangar where a yellow truck with adjustable stairs mounted on its side was driving out, turning in the direction of the new arrival.

The jet stopped, turbines winding down. The co-pilot, a small-framed black Cuban gentleman with a puff of gray for hair, exited the cockpit and opened the main door. The cabin depressurized with a subtle, hollow sensation, an impossibly huge breath being exhaled. The truck parked with its stairs aimed with practiced precision, raised them to the jet's door. The hydraulic pump under the stairs cycled loudly, an oily whine that resonated over the distant boking of startled chickens and oinking of hungry pigs. El Maestro stepped out and down the steps with his customary patience and collective, analyzing glances in all directions.

"*Hola*, Marcela," El Maestro greeted the stair truck driver, a sixtyish Mexicana with slicked back hair and a charming, toothless smile that pushed her cheeks out wide. He walked past the vehicle and turned to face the two men who were jogging from the hangar to meet their employer. Tall with dark buzz cuts and thick mustaches, both muscle heads wore blue mechanic's coveralls with patches on the top pockets that named them as Erik and Felix.

They stopped in front of El Maestro. "*Hola*, El Maestro," Felix said, smiling briefly. "*Como está?*" he asked.

El Maestro didn't respond right away. He stared into the distance, searching the dazzling horizon as if it held solutions to the troubles plaguing his current operations. Looking at his men, he acknowledged them with a curt nod, motioned for them to follow and walked toward the red brick building that squatted on the north side of its larger sibling, the main house, a brick villa well over two hundred feet wide. Spanish style doors and windows on both buildings were footed with small flower gardens that struggled to absorb moisture in the arid environment. El Maestro noticed movement in the garden mulch, a tiny scorpion that chased a spider twice its size into a patch of barrel cactus.

"Has the security team in Biloxi reported in today?" El Maestro asked, knowing everyone on the ranch awaited news on the murder investigation and gossiped about any updates, even after all this time. His loafers whispered over the stone walkway, silent steps that seemed to compound the heavy boots thudding behind him. A hot alkaline wind pulsed across the estate, dislodging sand from the dry, cracked dirt yard. The scent of manure stirred within the currents, at times so strong one had to hold their breath.

Erik glanced at Felix, then answered, "*Si, El Maestro. Esos Policios -*"

"Practice your English, Erik."

"*Si*, El Maestro. Those policemen say they no hear anything yet. Everyone has lost hope, and no more believe the policemen will find the traitor."

El Maestro nodded, muttered several brusque words. The mechanics shared a worried look, concerned about the irresolution not normally shown by their leader. Felix shrugged at Erik, said, "I can no believe El Maestro risk himself on the street."

"He wants to avenge Jose," Erik said, pride in his voice, defending the actions of his liege.

"*Si*. But now he wants to save that *gringa*. She deserved the honor, but this no good for him."

"*Ay, iy, iy,*" Erik breathed, shaking his head. "It is good to worry about El Maestro, but no good to question him."

"Enough from you two," El Maestro said, stopping in front of the ranch office. He opened the stained oak door. It opened quietly, weather seals brushing over the floor, allowing hot air to flow into the cold room. They walked inside. The mechanics sighed as the air conditioned coolness enveloped their overheated muscles, even cooler in places where sweat had accumulated.

The modern furniture was tasteful, businesslike, not overly expensive, as were the electronics that were visible. Consumer products that law enforcement raids would quickly dismiss as affordable on a rancher's income. Tall floor lamps stood behind a desk, a small sofa, and next to a chest-high bookcase, illuminating the room from the neck down, showing clean blue carpet and cream colored walls that looked new but smelled pleasantly well-lived in. El Maestro sat behind a large birch desk with a dull natural finish, leaned back in the padded swivel chair and interlaced his fingers over his belt. Eyeing his men with renewed irritation, he said, "Report."

Felix glanced at Erik, who nodded. Felix said, "The Gulfstream has another three hundred hours before the turbines need overhaul."

"Overhauling," El Maestro corrected.

"Overhauling. It will take one week."

"When?"

"We reviewed your traveling habits and estimated four months from now. Your secretary was informed for scheduling."

"Your English is improving, Felix," he praised, looked over at Erik. "And what of the ranch vehicles? Any repairs that exceed the usual maintenance costs?"

"No, El Maestro."

"Very well." El Maestro spun in his chair, grabbed a walkie-talkie out of its charger on top of the bookcase. He keyed it, spoke a request rapidly in Spanish, replaced it in the charger, chair creaking. A framed portrait hanging above the books caught his eye, riveting his feet and erecting his spine as he inhaled sharply from the grieving pain that attacked him once again. It was an artist's rendering of his long-time friend and business partner, Jose. A memorial drawn in pencil by a child in a poor village that was alive today because of Jose's compassion for his people.

Tears welled in El Maestro's eyes.

I am sorry I have not avenged you, *mi compadre*, he thought looking into the drawing's eyes and experiencing a sort of metaphysical connection. I will never stop searching for the *cabrone* that took your life and betrayed La Familia. And I will continue your charities, helping those that were unfairly wronged or simply deserving of a chance.

Like the girl.

I will help her, because that is what you would have advised me to do.

A tear trailed down his cheek. He pulled a hand-kerchief from his top pocket, yellow silk, perfectly folded. Wiped the tear, sniffing and turning back to his men. He said, "*Con permiso.*" Cleared his throat. "Now. Report, off the books." He interlaced his fingers again.

Felix went first, speaking with the excitement of a true gearhead. "The new go-fast boats are *mucho* better than the old models we had. Five-seventy-two big block Chevy engines, twelve hundred horsepower in each boat." He smiled, eyes widening, hands gesturing energetically with his words. "They are longer, with *mucho* payload capacity and upgraded navigation equipment that will temporarily jam the Coast Guard's radar."

El Maestro pursed his lips thoughtfully, nodded. He waved a hand at Erik.

Erik took a deep breath, concentrating on his second language. "The ATVs were equip with—"

"Equipped."

"*Gracias.* Equipped with infrared lamps for night vision driving in the desert. They now have ten-gallon reserve tanks, and we experimented with small trailers to pull behind them, but they were no good. Too clumsy over the terrain. Instead, we fabricated larger luggage racks and cut the seats to accom-, accomo—"

"Accommodate."

"*Gracias.* Accommodate the racks. They now carry one-third more product, and they get two-thirds more range."

"Very well. Good work. On the English, too."

A double tap sounded at the door. El Maestro nodded and Erik got up to open it. A thirty-something Mexicana in a maid's uniform of soft pink walked in, pushing a vacuum cleaner in front of her. She gave a brief bow for her boss, avoiding eye contact and ignoring the mechanics, who were shooting appreciative looks at her legs. She found a receptacle on a wall, plugged in her machine.

Before she could turn it on, El Maestro held up a hand to give her pause, waved for her to come to him, a specific motion that conveyed a specific meaning. She rolled the vacuum up to his desk, around it, stood it next to his chair. He turned to face it and unlatched a plastic panel on the front. The cover popped off and revealed an iPad integrated inside, a factory-quality installation. Turning it on, he used the touchscreen to scroll through coded files only he and the corporate maids were versed in. After several minutes of browsing, he grunted ambiguously, gestured at the screen inviting elaboration.

The maid bowed again, moved around the machine and squatted down to read the encrypted language. "*Inglés?*" English, she asked.

"Yes, please."

"Profits on the books will cover the maids', mechanics', and *rancheros'* salaries. Maintenance costs for the jet and airstrip have not yet been calculated, but projections show those expenses will make your personal salary miniscule." El Maestro waved a hand, unconcerned. She continued, scrolling through the files. "Livestock markets are unchanged. Off the books profits for this quarter were as expected, though I'm predicting the next quarter will be slightly below our target due to inefficient logistics." She cleared her throat. "*Senor* Jose's replacement is not as effective as we are used to." She bowed her head. Crossing herself, she murmured a quick prayer in Spanish for her late underboss, kept her head down, awaiting further instructions.

El Maestro's face flushed with sudden anger, a fleeting change that danced over him, head to toe, before vanishing from ruthless suppression. Equilibrium regained, he took a calming breath and looked at her. "Thank you, Elena. Notify the maid's team leader that I want encryption software upgraded every ninety days from now on. Every iPad and laptop in every company with off-the-books income. Several of the cartels have employed hackers, and I fear our current truces hold no sway in the virtual world."

"*Si*, El Maestro."

"That is all. Thank you, Elena."

The maid/accountant turned off the iPad, replaced the plastic panel and began vacuuming the already spotless floor.

PART IX

Central Mississippi Correctional Facility
Pearl, Mississippi
December 24, 2011

"IS THAT WEED you're smoking? I haven't smelled that stuff in years," I told my cubicle mate, Patty, who sat on her bottom bunk amid a cloud of reefer smoke.

"Yep," she replied, a puff wheezing out from the huge hit she held in.

"I thought you were going to church. For the big Christmas deal."

"I am," she shrugged. "I like to catch a good buzz before I pray. Gets me closer to Jesus."

I laughed, watching her face change colors from no oxygen. Unable to hold it in any longer, she gave a loud expulsion that curiously emitted little smoke, most of it apparently absorbed in her bloodstream by cavernous lungs. She stood up, smiling, eyes squinted nearly closed in pleasure, steel bed popping its released tension, swayed a little. Over six-feet with a large waist and brawny arms, very white skin with freckles and shining blonde hair that fell in waves just below her shoulders, Patty was a formidable woman. Smart, funny, and capable. I liked her from the moment we met.

My other cube mate was a different story, however. Yolanda sat up on the top bunk above Patty. Slim with protruding cheekbones, long dark hair and acne scars on her brown skin, the young Ecuadorian cocked her neck a few times with attitude, said to me, "You've changed."

"They say prison will do that to a girl," I responded with

attitude of my own.

"You used to be nice and understanding. Ever since you got a reputation, you've been judgmental."

"Reputation? Judgmental? No, Yolanda. I just call it like I see it. You're a fucking leech. If you can't pay me back, just say so. Don't connive over a few dollars in canteen. Good way to get your head busted."

"Wow," Patty said. "You have changed."

"You're just high," I said.

"True," Patty agreed, then started pinching the muffin top that hung over the waistband of her black and white pants. She sucked in her stomach. "Am I like really fat, or can I make the pathetic claim that I'm 'big boned'?" she asked me, turning like she was trying to find a skinny angle.

"Oh, Patty. Your body has to be big, to be able to hold such a big heart," I assured her, smiling. "Large and lovely."

She returned my smile, eyes glittering with merriment. And quality weed. "That's the nicest way I've ever been called fat. Thank you."

"You're welcome."

She sat down again, opened her locker box and took out a giant Honey Bun. Closed the box, unwrapped the pastry. Noticing my smirk, she told me, "Hey. Fat people have to eat, too."

"What about the church service? Don't they have food?"

"Damn. I forgot. I need to get going," she said, stuffing the Honey Bun in her mouth and standing up. "I'll eat there, too," she mumbled around the bun.

"What are you having?"

"Traditional hooker meal."

"Traditional?" I inquired.

Walking away, she turned her head, swallowed, and said, "Two missionaries in a sandwich."

I laughed, then yelled after her. "Don't molest those holy men. They'll stick your crazy ass under the prison!"

Yolanda and I giggled for a moment, then remembered we were beefing and resumed our antagonizing mugs. She sniffed, stuck her nose up and looked away from me.

I sighed. "We'll talk later. I'm off to clean toilets. I think."

"I thought you were sweeping and mopping."

"I'm not sure. The Latin Queens got me a job in the lockdown unit. Sounds thrilling, whatever it is."

"Well, there aren't that many jobs. And there are too many hoes trying to work. You should feel fortunate."

"Yeah, fortunate. That's what I feel."

Closing my locker box, I secured the lock, stood and walked past a pouting Yolanda to tell the tower officer I had to go to work. After leaving my ID with the CO, I walked out of the building and down several walkways before the unit I was looking for came into view. Heavy rain clouds seemed poised over its roof. A promise of ruining the rest of the day by canceling yard-call and other outside activities, potentially causing an institutional lockdown if the storm proved furious enough.

Cold wind blasted from the gray morning sky. Goose bumps prickled my arms, making me regret my decision to leave my jacket. I had planned to work hard to stay warm, but that wouldn't work out very well if I froze before getting there. I walked faster.

The lockdown unit was legendary on the compound, having a long history of horror stories. Beatings, stabbings, self-mutilating psych patients. As the main entrance buzzed and I walked inside, I sensed anxiety that was not quite hidden in the body language of the COs that meandered the halls and loitered by the tower doors. They bantered with each other, loudly, laughing and appearing at ease, but their quick glances at unlatching door locks and nervous eating of too much snack machine food showed the constant fears they dreaded. Of being fired for opening the wrong cell door, getting stabbed or scalded, or having feces thrown on them by a disturbed woman who has no qualms about engaging in biological warfare.

Real fears, from real experiences.

I've actually seen a CO that had been scalded with sugar water. It wasn't pretty, let me tell you. Her normally dark skin was blistered white, pink in places where the skin had completely melted off. And I've seen COs walk out of here with their heads down, dejected, after being fired for opening cell #153 when it should have been #152, causing a brutal stabbing and ending any future career in correctional facilities. Those sorts of incidents and the people involved in them were talked about for a week or so, then forgotten. A common occurrence not worth dwelling on. A terrible one, sure. But no one wanted to remember it.

For some reason, I didn't feel sorry for the officers. None of the COs took an interest in me, as usual. I wasn't feeling any urge to gain recognition or ask one of the idiots for instructions, so I went down the hallway between the zones looking for the door marked STORAGE, knowing all these buildings were of the same basic design. I found it quickly. Pushed it open. Mops and brooms stood haphazardly behind boxes of paper towels and detergents, bottles of industrial strength cleaner. Stepping inside the small room, I held my breath. There were dozens of chemicals and no telling how many molds and fungi vying for a chance to lay spores in my lungs. I pulled the collar of my shirt up over my nose and mouth, grabbed a yellow mop bucket and hurriedly filled it with hot water from the filthy porcelain sink that clung to the back wall like a drunken bum, slouched, crooked and beat up. Grabbed a packet of liquid detergent and squeezed it into the steaming water. Suds and bubbles popped, adding fresh fumes to the tiny room, making me sneeze several times. I grabbed a mop and broom at random, backpedaled the hell out of there, gasping deeply at the much cleaner air in the hallway.

Rolled the bucket to the A zone door, waved at the tower. It buzzed, clicked, and slid open with mechanical complaint. I walked through.

The zone had sixty cells, thirty in a horseshoe shape downstairs, thirty upstairs. My job was to clean the dayroom floor and tables, the upstairs tier floor, and stay away from the cells. No problem.

As I went about my mindless work, I thought about the months since I met Ignacio. Or El Maestro. Whatever the hell he calls himself. His influence had certainly made my life in prison more interesting. That dude was a legend among the street savvy, which was the entire population of this joint, including the officers. Word of our visitation showdown got around fast. I mean, it was like a mass text message hit the hundreds of contraband phones in every unit with the details, elevating my status to instant criminal celebrity. The weird thing is, I kind of like it. I've missed fame, I'm not ashamed to admit. This deal here is deep in the infamous spectrum of fame, but hey. I'm rocking it.

I remember walking back from visitation that day and passing other inmates who stepped away from me, making sure to maintain a respectful distance. And walking by officers that looked at me nervously but neglected to question my intended destination. Pretended I wasn't there.

Of course, by that point I looked like a stunt double for The Poltergeist, and would probably frighten Charles Manson with a glance. So maybe I'm assuming too much. Maybe they hadn't known so fast.

But they sure knew now, even if they didn't recognize me in my non-psychotic persona.

Finished with the broom, I dipped the mop in the bucket, in the soapy water that instantly turned brown from the repulsive mop head.

"That's just wrong," I grumbled, thinking about how unorganized this place was, that they couldn't even clean up a mop before storing it. I'll be here all day working on this damn floor. Well, it's either this or getting stuck on the zone listening to all the incredibly loud stupidity between groups of women. *One Life to Live* discussions. Screaming, card slamming games. My Baby Daddy A Loser drama.

Excedrin Headache #976,860,000.

Deciding this was a comparable heaven, I placed the mop in the wringer, leaned all of my one-hundred-and-thirty-five pounds on the lever and squeezed the Mississippi mud out of the old, thin cotton strings. The plastic and springs groaned loudly, echoing off the brick walls and steel doors, acoustics that reverberated as if this were an amphitheater.

The zone was full of women, every cell occupied. I caught several of them staring at me, or ducking out of their windows when I looked up. A few waved, most just gave me blank or nasty looks. I gave the same response to all of them. A simple nod, civil, not friendly, just a girl doing a slave job for a day off her sentence as payment.

I've been in this same unit several times for fighting officers (which, on reflection, makes me incredibly lucky to even have this job, and eligibility for Good Time), so I'm familiar with disrupting the orderly running of the institution and doing dungeon time. The women here couldn't make it in general population for many reasons. Fighting, robbing, extorting the weak. Or just getting in touch with their inner dumbass because they were bored. Several were on protective custody to be sheltered from such predatory behavior.

Not an ideal place to do time. Or work.

The mop plopped wetly on the floor. As I swirled and swayed with the strokes of cleaning, I hummed an unknown number, a tune written by happy thoughts, and imagined what Yolanda would look like wearing a Ringside Products t-shirt. Her peanut head would make a fine double-end bag.

I could trick her into thinking we were going to workout together...

Then I would start hitting her, and, too late, she would realize that she was the workout.

Hee-hee.

I stepped backwards and swung the mop as far as I could to either side, being careful not to get too close to the cells. My Yolanda workout plan almost got me doused with coffee and juice, thrown by two childish black girls in neighboring cells, laughing like they were teasing a smaller kid on a playground, giggling and slapping their thighs in the safety of their cells, unable to cogitate further consequences. Freaking ignoramuses. Definitely in touch with their inner dumbass.

I ground my teeth but ignored them, quietly thanking my quick reflexes and placing them at the top of my Proud Attributes list, which dropped my glutes to the #2 spot for the first time ever. (Sorry Perfect Booty. Survival trumps the self-esteem ya gave me). Threats and crap like that came at me during previous visits here. It seemed it would increase in frequency now that I was working the floor and had become a kind of sport for the arrested development windbags. For whatever reason, all these tough, hard black women couldn't stand to see a little ol' white chick trying to make this bacteria pit look and smell better. So much racism and tribalism was new to me. It was irrational, and really frustrating.

Stupid.

I grinned and hummed louder through my clenched teeth, imagining Ringside t-shirts on all these crazy bitches, more of them joining in now that the first salvo had been thrown. I swayed and swirled, dancing with the feeling of the pleasant fantasy. Added a few la-dee-da lyrics to my inane jam, shouting melodiously in response to the derogatory comments. Once they realized I wasn't fun anymore, they quit.

Hey, I can out crazy bitch any crazy bitch. Sometimes you have to fight fire with fire. Stupid with stupider.

Walking back to get the bucket, I passed a cell that had an enormous head filling the window. The light was on, barely peeking through gaps around the hippopotamus face in silhouette, whites of eyes the only thing distinguishable. Jeepers creepers, it was abnormal. I couldn't help looking again. The hippo bared its teeth at me, then punched the crap out of the steel door. It thundered like a bass drum throughout the zone, startling some of the women, who jumped away from their windows. Shouts for quiet followed.

"You shut up!" the hippo hollered back.

"Who that is? That you, Boogerilla?" someone a few cells down said, speaking through their tray slot.

"Yeah. That me," the hippo replied, thumping her door again. "This white bitch be looking me all in my face. Like she wanna fuck me, or some shit."

"Excuse me?" I said, standing up straight, unconsciously gripping the mop like a weapon.

"Who that is?" the tray slot said again.

"This white-bread nothing in front of my cell," Boogerilla said.

"What you be, girl?" the tray slot said, demanding to know what gang I represented.

"I'm just me," I responded.

"Oh. You nothing then."

Leaning the mop against a wall, I walked down to the talking tray hole, squatted down and looked into the eyes of a very rough featured black woman that could have been twenty-five or fifty-five. Scars ran thickly down one side of her face and continued even thicker across the contours of a shoulder and down the arm. Battle wounds from innumerable knife fights in here and on the street. I liked the scars, and she had some boss corn row braids. But I held my compliments.

I could see she and I were to be unfriendlies.

I let her get a good look at the beast lurking behind my eyes, then told her, "Oh, you can believe I'm something."

She narrowed her eyes. "I remember you now, small fry. You just left here. I know you supposed to be some big shot fighter in a ring with gloves. But I don't use gloves, small fry." Her hands out of sight, she grinded something heavy and metallic on the concrete floor. "I use iron," she breathed, then held up a length of metal longer than my hand, angle iron that I guessed came from the inside of a fluorescent light housing. She licked the blade, staring into my eyes.

Unimpressed, I told her, "If you call me a nothing again, you may have to use that flimsy piece of tin."

Outrage rippled across her features, deeply insulted that I would speak ill of her life's work. I walked away and she screamed at my back, "You dead, small fry! Nobody insults Chiquita like that. I make the best blades. The best!"

"I'll get her ass, Chiquita," Boogerilla said, hippo eyes alight as I walked past her cell again to grab the mop. "This door gonna swing one day while she be in the zone. Them tower officers always push the wrong buttons. That's how I got Mimi. I'll get this white bread ho, too. Only a matter of time."

I stopped and looked over at her, tilted my head. "What does Boogerilla mean, anyway? Booger gorilla? Your mother must be so proud."

"I'm going to kill you and fuck your dead body," she promised me, punching the door hard enough that I had to catch myself from flinching. Someone upstairs squeaked.

I grinned at her. "I hope you have a big one so my spirit will fly away with a satisfied smile."

"You think this is a game, bitch. You see. You will see."

The hippo disappeared, allowing light to show through the window. As I rolled the mop bucket to the stairs so I could go up and clean the top tier, I overheard Boogerilla talking to herself. Telling an imaginary friend what she would do to me. And I heard, actually felt, the hard grinding of a fresh piece of steel inside Chiquita's cell. A blade that would most certainly have my name on it.

Super-duper.

Not bad for my first day, huh?

"Carter!" a CO yelled at me from the zone door.

I turned to look. "Yeah?"

"Visitation. Let's go," she said, turning to speak to the tower officer.

Grabbing the broom and mop, I pushed the bucket behind the officer to the storage room, tiny wheels squeaking as I mulled over comparisons with previous jobs I've had, finding none. I made more enemies here in an hour than I have in my entire life. At least I got to knock off work early.

Merry freaking Christmas to me.

~ ~ ~

This place has a way of deluding a mind, forcing a person to think and behave, conform, to the tribal conditions. Lord of the Flies comes to mind. Civilized people isolated, unable to use the higher evolved thought processes that are needed to survive in the social realms of the free-world. Those processes I once used daily have regressed, commandeered by the primeval fight-or-flight life I live now, and shutting out any distractions that may hinder its mechanism.

Like my family. The most distracting element that could lessen my chances for survival in prison.

I have been so immersed in the institution that I haven't thought about what really matters in months. I haven't been able to. And I hated myself for it.

My extraordinary, beautiful goddamn family. How could I forget about them? I felt like a traitor.

I walked fast to the visitation room. Stood by impatiently as the CO that had escorted me signed the log on the desk and the visitation officer, the same jacked up dune buggy booty with Popeye's grease face that's always there, buzzed me into the room. My mother, father, and my trainer, Eddy, sat behind a table with huge inviting smiles. I stopped in my tracks, stunned by the beautiful sight, rushing with pleasure that made me glow a pure smile in return, chest tightening, making it a conscious effort to breathe, aggressive persona taking a hiatus, a sensation I felt physically, as if a part of my soul had gone into another room to give us some privacy.

Hella surreal, man.

Faces and memories flashed, seemingly in front of my eyes. A 3D movie where graphic scenes from my past jumped out at me through red and blue shades, filtering my vision. Dug up from a neuronal tomb where I stuff all the information that makes me feel like screaming, stifled and sad and head-banging-on-a-table pissed the fuck off.

I hate feeling like that.

So I choose not to, and can usually pull it off successfully. Or rather, Shocker can. But there's a penalty when it all comes flooding back, like it was now.

It hurts.

Like a mother'.

"Hi," I said, a loud whisper in the quiet room. Even the building was silent. None of the usual bumps, bangs and distant jibing from trustees pretending to work. Crashing silence. Their chairs scraped the floor as all three of them stood up, walked quickly around the table to give me a group hug.

Mom took charge and backed the men out of the way. "Clarice! You look dreadful," she greeted me with her usual criticism, touching my cheeks, hair, turning my head for inspection, fussing over her daughter as I grinned and tingled at her touch.

Damn, that felt good. I realized I have really missed this wonderful woman. The aromas of home permeated her, releasing a flood tide of even more memories. These more pleasant, thankfully.

An inch shorter than my five-eight, Jade Ares was the epitome of class. She was petite, handsome rather than pretty. Sported fashionable, short-styled blonde hair touched with the perfect mix of gray. Pro makeup highlighting her bright green eyes and high cheekbones, subtly diminishing the piggy nose that was the progenitor of mine. Cosmetically enhanced lips that belied her fifty-nine years, glossed clear-of-pink. Thousand dollar green pantsuit, conservative black heels that knocked repeatedly on the floor as she walked around me, scowling at my appearance, harrumphing.

How could anyone not love this woman? She was a hundred-and-twenty pounds of Make You Feel Good.

"Nice to see you, too, Mom," I croaked. Turned to look at my father. He stood next to Eddy, watching his wife do her mother hen bit with pride emanating from every part of his body. Danny Ares was equal in height with Eddy, fifty pounds lighter, sixty with dark brown dyed hair. Ridiculous green bowling shirt he probably wore to please Mom in a color matching couple's scheme. It covered a small paunch that will earn him a lecture from his daughter if it gets any bigger. Blue jeans and wing-tipped Doc Marten's. A lifetime coffee drinker, his unceasing smile shone like ivory rather than porcelain. Brown eyes squinted on his craggy face, distinguished with laugh lines and crow's feet. I wanted to kick myself for not thinking about this loving, loyal man every second of every day.

My chest tightened even further. My boobs ached. But it felt awesome.

Mom completed her inspection, signaling the men that

they were allowed to come forward again. Eddy stood back, anxiously awaiting his turn. He looked like a big bulldog told to stay away from his favorite toy, fidgeting with impatience.

"It's so good to see you, Clarice. Merry Christmas," Dad said, hugging me, twisting side-to-side. He smelled like a forest in the winter, clean and sharp. But he felt like the comfort of a day at the beach with a bottle of wine. His soft businessman's hands cupped my chin. "They treating you okay?"

Before I could answer Eddy's patience took that as a cue to vacate and he plowed my dad out of the way, grabbing me with arms that felt like they wrapped around me twice. Squeezed me in a crushing grizzly hug. Lifted me off the floor like a sack of feathers. My smile was mostly a painful grimace.

"I think we should ask if she is treating them okay," Eddy rumbled in his basso voice, under bite stuck out, grinning. My feet reacquainted with gravity. I grinned back at him, hugging his U.S.A. Team jacket, which felt looser on him.

Stepping back and indulging my own inner Mother Hen, I grabbed his arm and turned him, like I was deciding whether to label him Accepted or Failed.

He didn't pass.

"You've lost weight," I told him, then sniffed. "Though I don't see how. Your breath smells like fried oysters."

"Yes. No. I haven't noticed," he said, dismissing my attention to his eating habits. "I've missed you, girl. Come on! Let's see that jab." He held up his meaty paws, big as punch mitts, and started moving around me in a circle with an intent expression.

I laughed, automatically stepping into a boxing stance and lunging at him with rapid jabs that popped like thunderclaps on his palms, causing Mom to stick her fingers in her ears. My muscles stretched and swelled with power. I felt like a racehorse that had been left in the stables for too long, bursting with the need to go, the need for speed.

I doubled up, really clowning, feeling my monster start to rock, sticking his hand mitts with lightning stabs of my left fist, pivoting, weaving, lunging in and out. Shoes chirping on the floor. We laughed together, immersed in the movements that have been so intrinsic to our lives, responsible for so many joyful challenges and emotional moments of achievement. Cornerstones. Larger than life experiences.

A snarl gripped my lips. Killer instinct surfacing and taking control of my feet, stomping hard into a power jab, booming into his hand. Eddy roared with laughter, shaking the room like Pavarotti in a concert hall. I dropped below his hands and tagged his stomach with a five-punch combination that was almost too fast for ears to distinguish, sounding like a single blow. An ability I could do without the weight of hand wraps and gloves on my fists. I grabbed my trainer's waist and hugged him again. Nostalgic tears pooled in my eyes as the faint smell of boxing gyms crinkled off his jacket. Punching, jumping, grunting sounds seemed to accompany it.

Mom sobbed behind us. Grabbing her side for a purse that wasn't there, retained by an officer in the front where visitors come in. Tissues absent, she used the sleeve of her jacket to staunch her tears before her face became completely mussed. I let go of Eddy and hugged her again.

"I missed you," I told her, rubbing her back and burying my cheek in her bosom. A nagging thought occurred to me. Like a smack in the face, I realized the person I wanted to see the most, needed to see, wasn't there. "Where's Nolan?" I said. My son was staying with my parents while his were incarcerated.

Dad stepped between us, answered, "He refused to

come. We tried everything, believe me. But he wouldn't get in the car. Regina is watching him," he said, referring to their housekeeper. He looked suddenly uncomfortable, cleared his throat. Sat down in a plastic chair.

"He said you aren't his mother and he never wants to see you again," Mom sobbed, sniffing, hiding her face behind her hands. "He said you broke your promise to never leave again."

"Now, Jade. That's not-" Dad began.

Mom dropped her hands and glared at him through tears and eyes of fire. An expression alien to her facial muscles, absurdly incongruous. "She deserves the truth, Danny. You always want to sugar coat!"

Eddy and I looked back and forth between the couple we've never witnessed in disagreement before, appalled at the outburst. It showed just how screwed up things had become because of my husband and me being wrongfully imprisoned. It showed how much I've missed because of infrequent communication, how unaware I've been of how everyone connected to me has been deeply affected.

It was unsettling to say the least.

Eddy noticed my horrified look and whisked me away, grabbing my shoulders and marching me across the room to give my parents a chance to regain composure and speak to me in confidence. His baritone whisper felt like a ginormous bumblebee in my ear. "I was contacted by the Teacher," he said.

"What? Why?" I stuttered. A horrific feeling quickly took over the bliss I was enjoying.

"He explained his involvement in your case and wanted to help however he could."

"Okay. And?"

"And he sent me documents for you. Had a former colleague of mine deliver them. An old trainer I knew from Mexico. Two sets of driver's licenses, social security cards and birth certificates. Plus twenty large in cash," he bumble bee-ed in my ear, glancing at my parents to see if they were listening. They were whispering in a furious argument, heads bowed together, pointing fingers all around for emphasis.

I looked back at Eddy and closed my stunned mouth. It fell open again. "No shit?" was the best I could come up with. IDs? Cash? My head spun with the possibilities.

"Yeah. After I got over my urge to hurt that guy, I got to liking him - he's my kind of people - and agreed to help. Your folks know about this, but not about the documents and money. No one else needs to know the names on the IDs. And your poor folks can't handle too much involvement in underground activities, anyway. That's my forte." He chuffed and smirked, a quirk he used to do before brokering less-than-ethical deals during my boxing career. He had always shielded me from the shady side of the fight game, keeping my hands and image squeaky clean. Apparently, he was doing the same for my mom and dad now. He continued, "With the passports, you can get on a plane to anywhere in the world. The Teacher offered the same deal for Ace. But you have to get out first."

"All right. I'll do some homework and get back to you. What are the names on the IDs?" I asked, curiosity getting the better of me.

He frowned in thought. "Patricia on one. Connie on the other. I think. Cute, huh?" He waggled his heavy brows.

"I don't know. I don't trust the Teacher."

"I understand. Just let me know. In the meantime, we can plot the rest of it." He inclined his head at my parents. "Danny has something for you."

"What?" I said, turning to look at my dad.

"A cellphone," he answered, grinning. "Untraceable. Also courtesy of the Teacher."

"My dad brought a phone in here?" I said incredulously.

My damn mouth was going to catch flies at this rate.

"Yep. Said he wanted to be the one to take the risk."

"That's insane!" I said too loudly. Mom and Dad stopped their fuming and looked over at us. Eddy clapped me on the shoulder and we walked back over to their table, sat down. They followed suit, both of them pressing elbows on the table, leaning toward me.

I looked at Dad. "You, um, need to tell me something?" I asked hesitantly. Weird didn't begin to describe what I felt. The thought of my father, a Christian do-gooder, committing a felony was dumbfounding. I've never heard of him breaking any rules, much less serious laws.

My dad? Heh. Right.

"Yes," he said, clearing his throat. He glanced at Mom, then at the CO through the window, who sat at the desk, flipping through a magazine. He continued, whispering, "The Teacher called your mother and me. We want to help."

"But you could go to jail if you get caught," I whispered back in protest.

He held up a hand. "You were sentenced to forty years, Clarice. Forty. Years." He paused, tears glazing his steely eyes. "I won't stand by and let you waste your life in here if I can do something about it," he said, emotion flushing his face, love and passion for his only child. Mom patted his hand. "Well, I can do something about it. I was able to get past the metal detector because of the screws and pins in my leg. Your mother brought a medical report to prove it. Hang on a minute." His arms disappeared under the table. The room silent once more, his zipper peeling open was very loud. I almost laughed.

A moment later, the tearing, ripping sound of strong tape pulling hair from skin grew loud in the room. His face turned a deep, painful scarlet as he held back an outcry. I cringed at the sound and the excruciating look on Dad's normally pleasant face. And the image of my father's pubic hair stuck all over a phone he was about to hand me. Eddy also cringed, hands ducking under the table, likely holding his junk in sympathy. Mom looked around guiltily, embarrassed, panicked. A range of reactions piqued by her morals from the blatant violation of the laws she had so loyally abided by up until this day.

I nearly choked, holding back laughter. Yeah, weird couldn't possibly describe it.

Dad's shoulders jerked a few more times and he bent over so his face almost touched the table. Rouge with hues of violet throbbing around veins in his temples, on his creased forehead. The poor man looked like he needed a stool softener in a bad way. A final jerk and his hands bumped hard into the underside of the table. He gave a grunt of surprise and something plastic clattered loudly on the floor. Four sets of eyes bugged out around the table. Mom squeaked, totally wigged out.

At that moment, the CO from the visitation desk walked in, ushering another inmate. The inmate, a white chick with greasy, stringy hair, maybe thirty years old with meth addiction written all over her abused body, spotted the phone and immediately pointed it out to the officer. Snitched on us. My stomach joined my jaw, bungee jumping to the floor. My parents' responses mirrored mine, but Eddy was on a different level about the whole situation.

As the snitching slut pointed out the contraband on the floor, the CO maneuvered through the doorway and looked where the phone lay, eyes popping even more than ours. Looked up at Eddy and jerked back from the murderous stare he directed at the snitch, at her, back to the snitch. Eddy sprang up a second later, chair flying out behind him as if he threw it. He snarled at the tattletale, then flipped the table over in her direction, roaring in anger, the booming rage vibrating my head, blurring my vision. The officer and inmate screamed in terror, piercing shrieks that would have more officers in here faster than any emergency code shouted into a walkie-talkie could accomplish. Their shaky legs propelled them against a wall, where they huddled together for perceived safety.

Everyone watched in stunned disbelief as Eddy swiftly grabbed the phone from between my dad's feet and sprinted to the restroom, his speed and agility for such a large man doubling the stun factor. The men's room door banged open. A toilet flushed.

A prison toilet. With enough flushing power to suck down a small dog. Brilliant!

Eddy had disposed of the evidence, his quick thinking and even quicker action had saved my dad from a potential five years in prison for introducing contraband into a correctional facility.

Whew, fuck, what???

A sort of relieved vertigo overcame me, allowing me to breathe again. As Eddy walked out of the restroom, still snarling, disgusted, glaring dangerously, footsteps and excited walkie-talkies approached from behind the hyperventilating CO and frightened snitch.

Mom sobbed. Dad held his hands over his face. I banged my head on the table.

PART X

South Mississippi Correctional Facility
Leaksville, Mississippi
January 5, 2012

THE CONCRETE FLOOR was cold as the man laid his bare back down on it to stretch. Wearing white boxer shorts and prison issue shoes of poor quality, new but already creased and torn, Alan "Ace" Carter extended his long arms over his head, inhaling deeply. Stretching his diaphragm with a yoga method, holding for a count of eight, releasing and exhaling for another eight. Forcefully deflating his lungs for another few seconds, oxygenating his muscles in preparation for a workout.

Sitting up he reached for his toes, knees locked, continuing the deep breathing, grabbing his heels and burying his face between his knees. He exhaled and groaned with pleasure as his hamstrings loosened, burning with a gratifying sensation.

"If I could do that, I'd never leave my bed," lisped a man walking into the four-bed cubicle. Tall and as slim as Ace, Diamond paused to look at his friend, one hand on a hip encased in too-tight striped pants, the other bent at the wrist in a dainty, feminine posture. His yellow-brown skin glowed with moisturizers that weren't sold on the canteen, accentuating a wide nose and wider smile on a handsome, mid-twenties face. Shaved eyebrows replaced by pencil liner makeup. Red bandana styled like origami on his head, knotted in the front.

Ace laughed and flipped over to do some pushups. "Yeah, right. If you could do that, your freaky ass would get rich in the porn business," he said, grunting as he finished a set of twenty.

"As I said. I'd never leave my bed." Diamond giggled playfully before sitting on his bottom bunk, watching Ace's lanky, ripped physique with platonic admiration. He'd long since given up on the fantasy of them together as a romantic couple, happily resigned to having him as a friend and confidant.

Ace started another set, but faltered as the image his friend evoked settled in his mind like an uninvited guest, funny, though a little off-putting. Snickering, he forced his arms to pump again.

"What are you two dummies doing?" an officer said, stopping in front of Ace, High-Tech boots clumping, indicating a weight deceptive to his appearance. He looked at Diamond. "You're supposed to be at work, not pitching woo on white boys," Lieutenant Cole said, crossing arms over a barrel chest. His black, almost blue face broke into a wide smile, teeth extremely white in contrast. His bald head shined under light coming through barred and screened windows. Cole fixed his eyes on Diamond with something more than good-natured amusement, waiting on a response he seemed to know would be tart.

Ace continued pounding out pushups, ignoring the exchange between the men he suspected would be lovers before long.

If they weren't already, he thought, smirking.

"Your black ass be all up in my Kool Aid and don't even know cherry from grape," Diamond sassed, turning his nose up, looking to the side and rolling his eyes with dismissal.

Cole's eyes seemed to grow brighter. "My black ass will bust through your wall like the Kool Aid man himself. I'll make you any damn flavor I want," he said, still beaming his smile. He uncrossed his arms like he intended to make good on his threat.

Ace stood up, eyes wide and near to bursting with laughter. He choked it down, said to them, "Uh. You two need a moment? I'll hit the yard and get my run in." He grabbed a t-shirt and black and white pants off his top bunk.

Cole crossed his arms again, turned to look at Ace. "No, big guy. I'll deal with this cocoa butter urn later," he said, jerking a massive thumb at Diamond, who wore a pleased expression behind Cole's back. Ace kept a carefully neutral look. "Right now, I need to talk with you." He spun around to Ace's cube mate again. "So you need to skedaddle to the yard."

Diamond uncrossed his legs, unhurriedly, stood with a shrewish look at Cole that said he would get away with ordering Diamond around this time but wouldn't be so fortunate the next round. Strutted out of the cubicle and down the center of the zone with a hand on his narrow hips, working his backside like a runway model. Cole watched with his big smile, appreciatively, eyes twinkling.

Diamond suddenly stopped, spun around with a smooth half-pirouette, knowing Cole would be looking, waved a hand in front of his face. "My-my-my-my poker face, nigga," he sang, cocking his neck side-to-side with his lyrics. He spun around again, resumed his strut to the end of the building and out an open door that exited onto the yard. Catcalls and loud greetings came through the doorway.

Ace's pent up laughter came rushing out.

"I think," he gasped, holding sore abs, "that he likes you." He wiped his eye before it teared.

Cole rumbled his own laughter, put his hands on his waist. "Yeah, that's my nigga." He looked around to see if anyone was near. The long rectangular steel building had cubicles lining both walls its entire length, all empty, the occupants at work or outside for recreation. The front of the zone had a small guard tower, security windows capped with a steel grate, caked with dust. A tiled area right in front of the tower had several showerheads on a wall. The clean tiles reflected the fluorescent lights, smelling strongly of bleach. The officer in the tower appeared to be sleeping, arms crossed on the control panel, head rested on top of them. Cole looked back at Ace. "I don't know what kind of business you were in on the street, but you have some powerful friends," he said.

Ace frowned at him. "I was a diagnostic specialist, at my wife's shop."

"Uh-huh. Look, big guy. I'm not the po-lice," he said, tapping the MDOC badge on his white lieutenant's shirt. "I'm a correctional officer. And I believe interacting with prisoners is the best way to make things run sweet around here. You feel me?"

"Sure."

"So you don't have to pretend to be innocent, or worry about me busting you for some petty bullshit. As long as niggas ain't robbing or jumping on the little guys, slinging shanks, I don't care what y'all do."

"Sounds good to me. But you should know that I am innocent. The arresting officers framed my wife and I. We got forty years, and we didn't do anything."

"Uh-huh," Cole repeated, bright smile showing once more. "Gee, I've never heard that before. And I've been here for eighteen years."

Ace looked down and shook his head, lifted his hands, dropping them in exasperation.

"That's cool, big guy. It's all good. Stick to your guns. We don't have to tell each other secrets to do business."

"Business?" Ace said, looking up quizzically.

"Here." Cole dug into a front pocket and pulled out a small bundle of brown paper towels, handed it to him. Ace looked around quickly, unwrapped the package to see what was inside. A Ziploc bag containing an iPod Touch, a credit card size Wi-Fi router and universal charger with USB wires shocked all the moisture out of his mouth. He couldn't believe the sight in his lap. His dry lips opened and closed with a question that wouldn't quite come out, only making a clicking noise in the silent cubicle.

Cole chuckled at his reaction. "That shit looks tight, but I don't know how you're gonna use it. That new cellphone jammer they put outside won't let any calls go out. I have to drive about two miles away before my phone will work," he said, eyeing the electronics with an expression that showed he knew very little about technology.

Ace's shaking hands hurriedly rolled the paper towels around the bag again. Licking his lips, he said, "That jammer will block the Three-G network almost completely. This," he indicated the package, "is a Mi-Fi router that works on the Four-G network, and has enough bandwidth to get around that jammer. The Four-G Long-Term Evolution is the best network."

"Guess your people knew that, huh? Can you make calls on it?"

"Yeah. The iPod connects to the Mi-Fi. You can download an app called Text free with Voice and make Internet calls. Or do it with the Skype app."

"Skype. I've heard of that."

"Social network. Mostly video chat and phone calls."

"Damn, big guy. You're in there," Cole said, holding his fist out for a bump. Ace obliged him and they smiled at each other. Cole stood up. "Better find a good hiding place. If K-Nine or ERT finds that your 'I am innocent' ass will go to lockdown for a good six months. Maybe catch a charge, too. That's a felony." He started to walk away, business finished. Another day at the office.

Ace stopped him. "Wait! Who gave you this?" He glanced around, lowered his voice. "I have to know."

Cole eyed him suspiciously for a few seconds. "You really don't know, do you?"

"Wish I did. I honestly don't know what the hell is going on. The last thing I expected was an officer to hand me an electronic felony."

Cole walked back to the cubicle and said, "You ever hear of El Maestro?"

"The Teacher? Heard of him, yeah."

"Big time cartel leader. Mexican guy. The Latin Kings around here idolize him. The real LKs, the Mexicans. Not those poor Mississippi white boys that got tricked into joining. Anyway. He pays well," he said, grinning and rubbing his index finger and thumb together.

"Latin Kings? Uh. I'm not Mexican. Or a tricked affiliate."

"I guess you are now, big guy. You just have to ask yourself if you're another poor Mississippi white boy that got tricked, or are you a business associate." Cole smiled, winked, then walked to the tower. He slapped a hand on the steel door. The startled officer inside jumped awake and buzzed the door open for the lieutenant. He walked through and the door clunked shut behind him.

The low roar of the ventilation motor and distant laughter of convicts outside playing softball reassured Ace that he had privacy, at least for the moment. He ran a hand through his close-cropped brown hair, blowing out a breath loudly. Glanced around for a place to stash the iPod and router, which seemed to burn with possibilities in his hands, heavy, full of promise. A hundred thoughts and emotions assaulted him all at once. His razor sharp mind prioritized each one.

I can call my son, he thought. Hell, we can video chat.

Smiling with anticipation of seeing Nolan's precious face on the touchscreen, several other scenarios rapidly overwhelmed his train of thought. His breathing and heart rate quickened, hands shaking, becoming vibrating instruments of multiple talents. Smile stretching to a grin, excitement from his dormant skills resurfacing to remind him of who he was and what he could do.

"I am the King of Hackers," he said.

Standing up, he clutched the package and began to pace back and forth between the bunk beds. Muttering, fingers twitching as if typing on a keyboard. There is plenty of lightweight hacking I could do with this baby, he pondered, recalling his old job at Wikileaks as their top hacker. Or "researchers" as they liked to title the position.

All those iPhones I broke into or cloned that belonged to top military brass - I could recite the specifications in my sleep! This iPod Touch has the same interface and software capabilities as an iPhone...

"Ha!" he gloated as more ideas occurred, mind racing faster as his hacker's criminal mind took over, making a mental checklist of larger systems the iPod could access and control for even larger hack jobs. I could get transferred to CMCF and be closer to Clarice. Or send her "legal mail" with any message I want, he considered, chest tightening at the thought of his wife.

I miss her so much!

An epiphany stopped him dead in his tracks, striking like a bullet, the train of thoughts colliding with an immovable wall of precedence. He now knew what must be done. What had to be done, and what was now possible because of the priceless fortune in his hands. Forget Skyping with Nolan. Or sending messages to Clarice.

I can be with them again, in person, he decided. I can organize an escape. Mine and hers.

A draft cooled the sweat that had appeared on his forehead. As he snapped out of his dazed contemplation, he started pacing again, muttering, "Son of a bitch. El Maestro, who the hell are you?"

PART XI

RUDE PEOPLE SUCK. I mean, mosquitoes show more courtesy than the ignoramuses that work here. At least they have a legitimate reason for their abusive behavior. These COs and administrators couldn't make that claim. Like this idiot pounding on my cell door right now. Wham! Wham! Like a Neanderthal with a tusk club. Ugh, me stupid cavewoman. Me no respect people. Ugh! Couldn't be a polite knock, a light civilized tap of inquiry.

No. Just bludgeon the damn thing and show your true stupid blue colors.

Idiot.

I briefly considered playing opossum. Like the psych patients do sometimes. Then again, that sort of childishness would only perpetuate the rudeness, drive up the impatience level. That's the reason they do it; they throw a blanket treatment over all of us, even the ones that don't cause any trouble, because past experiences with immature prisoners have drained them of patience and courtesy. Or, they are just mean.

Still, though. I don't agree with that treatment, or any form of group punishment. Especially when it's directed at me. So I lay in my bed ignoring the loud, vaguely female voice demanding I come to the door. Spite was one of my few indulgences these days, and this psych patient opossum stuff was kinda fun.

Smiling, I rolled over, pulled the sheet over my head

and said, "But I don't wanna go to school!"

"I'll write your ass up, convict! I'll make sure you get more lockdown time. Now bring your Lindsay Lohan-looking ass to this door!" she yelled.

Her fuming, spitting impatience gave me the petty gratification I needed, so I dragged the sheet off of me, stepped into my shower shoes and padded to the door. Squatted down to peek out the tray slot at the officer who was already in the top five of my Rude People That Suck list.

"What's your name, convict?" demanded a tall black woman with captain's bars on the shoulders of her white shirt. Her forehead appeared to bulge from a tight ponytail, a weave of long hair pulled severely away from an almost masculine face. Strong chin, clefted, long nose that extended in proportion to her forehead. Beady, creepy eyes. Her wide jaw muscles flexed as she smacked gum right in my face, bent over looking at me through the slot.

Smacking six inches from someone is rude and disgusting, don't you agree? Wet, juicy, popping smacks. And the gum wasn't doing anything to help her breath. Gross.

The thought must have telegraphed on my face. Her gaze narrowed sharply.

"Clarice Carter, J-one-three-three-two," I said, leaning back a little and holding my breath. Watching her mouth cycle like a cow chewing a cud. I closed my eyes and suppressed a shiver.

"You got your job back, convict," she said. Then spat a stream of thick brown juice that hit the floor with such volume it sounded like a spilled drink.

She was chewing freaking tobacco! What the hell? I don't recall ever seeing a woman with that nasty habit. It was beyond my comprehension as to how she could do that and still wear long hair, nails, and makeup.

Bizarre. My throat burned as I tried not to vomit. Eww.

"Um," I replied. "Great. I guess."

"Damn right it's great, convict. You can start by cleaning that shit up." She pointed at the tobacco spit.

My throat burned again, but with anger, heating my face and arms to the point I thought I would start emitting incandescent flares. "What's your name, Captain?" I growled, choking down several names that begged to form on my lips. I almost giggled, and the anger started to dissipate. Laughter really is the best medicine. Her eyes flashed and narrowed again.

"Correctional Commander Portsmouth," she growled back, managing to make it a snide remark. Like she wanted to offend me with it.

What the hell was this broad's deal?

"What's the deal?" I frowned, genuinely interested in her motives. Besides being a nut job, something else was off here. Didn't equate with the take-everything-and-lock-'em-down mentality that was the norm for crazy, lazy officers like her.

"What are you bumping your gums about convict?"

"How did I get my job back while I'm in lockdown? And do I call you 'Correctional Commander' or 'Captain'?"

"You get your job back because I say so. Getting caught trying to get a cell phone in ain't no thing. You ain't no security risk. And maybe I like seeing your little cream tail shaking behind a broom. Maybe I don't. And you can call me 'Commander' or 'Captain' because that's what I be doing to you. Commanding and Captaining," she said, talking louder as she finished, standing up straight and putting hands on hips. Thick gold and platinum blinged from every finger. She spat again for emphasis. Even her chewing got louder.

I failed to suppress the shiver this time. "Gosh, Captain. How can I refuse such a compelling personality?"

She shifted her weight to the other foot. Rolled her neck.

"You ain't got no choice, Cream Tail. Nam! Now shut your sporty mouth and get dressed. You start now." She spat again, this time on my door, covering my tray hole with tobacco ick. Bubbles stewed in dark, stinking saliva. She walked away. A moment later her boots thumped heavily down the stairs. The zone door buzzed open, slammed shut behind her. I let out a long sigh and grabbed a pair of yellow pants out of my locker box. Lockdown wear. I slipped them over men's boxer shorts I wore like most of the other women did, white Bob Barker deals that hung to my knees and always embarrassed me by showing my panties through the penis access hole in the front.

Yep. This is what my life has become.

"Wrong. Just wrong," I muttered, looking around my cell and hating it. I actually felt glad to be able to clean up Captain Yuckmouth's mess just to be able to get the hell out of the cell and move around some. She knew that, too. She had my number. Just like I'm sure she treated everyone else she had leverage on. Probably does the same thing to her family.

Wow. I wonder if that thing has kids.

Nah. I doubt there's a man on this planet desperate or brave enough to hit that.

Feeling a little better with that façade of logic, I murmured a quick prayer for children I didn't know and hoped didn't exist, just in case. Slipped on my shoes and tucked in my shirt, shivering as a blast of wind seeped through my window. I turned and looked up at the vents above the door and smirked. My husband's farts blow warmer air than that heater. Piece of crap.

I opted to leave the yellow uniform top off, regulations be damned. I would rather freeze and risk a write-up than wear something that makes me look like a sack of potatoes (Tomboy, cute. Farmboy, no).

Peeking out of my tray slot again, across the zone at the

guard tower window, I searched for signs of movement that would indicate someone was awake and about their job. A silhouette moved. A big one, bigger than my upper body. Considering the diet and fashion in these parts, I determined it was just an obese woman's head with a cheap wig. I stuck my arm out and waved at it. "Hey! Officer in the tower! Let me out. I'm the floor walker!" I yelled, voice echoing as if I had shouted into a cave.

Several women came to their doors to investigate. The head in the tower bobbed up and down, looking in my direction. I think. My door buzzed, clicked, opened. I walked out into air that felt like a cold spring morning, but smelled like feet and ass. They certainly needed someone to clean up around here. I was happy to do it.

I do not like the way this is going.

My next step plopped into a puddle of spit, instantly staining the white canvas material my shoes were made of. "Yuckmouth bitch," I grumbled. "Lovely. Just fucking lovely."

Standing on one foot, I shook the other, slinging brown drool all over the floor. Giggles, then full-throated laughter pealed out of the cells on both sides of me. It was contagious. Really, this situation was so damn ridiculous I just had to laugh. I looked at my neighbors and grinned, shaking my head in a What Can I Do? gesture.

Downstairs a door boomed from a massive blow. A powerful strike from a huge arm, a fist that had to be callused like leather from such impacts all day and night. Tough girl posturing that could only come from one person.

"Boogerilla. You sexy hooker. You must have smelled me come out," I said as she struck the door again, walking past several cells on my way to the stairs. Women watched me from their windows or tray slots, oddly quiet, like animals that sensed a storm was on the way. I felt it, too. And wondered what would entice such distinctive intuition.

Whatever it was, it didn't feel good.

It felt like trouble. Serious, mean biker granny panties trouble.

Boogerilla punched her door again, then yelled out of her slot at the tower. "Hey Officer Abrams! Captain Portsmouth gave me a job, too. Let me out so I can clean the showers!"

Uh-oh.

I stepped to the handrail and looked down. A door buzzed open under me, the click of the heavy lock vibrating the metal under my hands, jolting my heart into a higher gear. My lungs took the cue, inhaling deeply to pump my muscles full of oxygen for fuel, bellows feeding a fire until it roared with extreme energy. The cool air around me heated slightly from thermal radiation as my whole body primed for fight mode. An instinctual process that was a warm, pleasant rush, tingling with heightened senses and a promise of explosive, scary movement that could only end badly for the person on the receiving end of it.

Goddamn, what a great FEELING!

My mouth clicked dry, my bladder felt full, and I knew I was ready. I knew what was coming. I've thought about it for weeks, ever since this booger bear first threatened me. Her and the other one, the knife maker. Chiquita. My fighter's mentality instantly analyzed them both and devised a game plan should they ever get a chance to make good on their threats.

Like right now.

A big girl like her will run into a lot of problems going up against a trained pro that's slicker and faster than her. She's a schoolyard bully, a brute that will throw wide, looping punches, easy to block or counter. Though I doubt I will have to do all that. If my plan works, she won't get to throw a single punch.

Boogerilla walked right past the mop bucket and

cleaning supplies she was supposed to be using. Grunted as her foot hit the first step and she started climbing, talking trash up the entire flight of stairs, boosting her confidence more than trying to scare me. She looked up at me and I was sure of my plan now. It would work.

Let her believe I'm scared to death. She'll underestimate me. And I'll Shocker.

Hee-hee. This will be fun.

"I told you, white-bread ho!" she bellowed up at me. "I told you I'd get your ass. It's on like Donkey Kong." She punctuated this prestigious statement with a crazy bark, a clipped explosion of her vocal cords that made someone squeak in a cell behind me. Hatred twisted her face into a god-awful snarl, lifting her wide, plump cheeks back like hackles on a mastiff, baring teeth with driving energy and combat readiness. Her hair was shaped in a tall, thick Afro, clumped down on one side, making her head and neck look gargantuan, otherworldly, a beast from a low budget B movie. She wore a yellow uniform top, no t-shirt underneath, the dark skin of her upper breasts showing through the V-neck, more of a chest than a bosom. Huge shoulders and arms that made the 5XL sleeves look like Spandex. Barrel-shaped torso with rolls of flab a Sumo wrestler would envy.

Sheesh.

Her legs were short, but each as big as my waist, pulsing under yellow pants like columns of animated marble. Stomping down on shoes that bulged on the outsides from at least two-hundred-and-sixty pounds threatening to rip them open with every step. I did a double take, focusing on her surprisingly small feet. They were wide, but short, abnormally out of proportion with her top-heavy body.

Yeah, she'll run into some problems. Literally.

"She'll come forward with no balance," I muttered, then backed away to initiate my plan. Eyes wide, I held up my hands, a frightened posture, pleading. I shook my head as if I couldn't believe this was happening and was about to pee in my panties. "NO!" I cried in a high-pitched shrill. "I'm sorry! I haven't done anything to you. Why are you doing this?"

Backing away along the tier, it was a chore to keep from laughing at myself. I could land an acting gig with this performance. Every cell door I passed had a head in the window. They stared, anxiously, excited about the drama unfolding and hoping it would become even more entertaining. A feeling I could relate to. It was boring in here.

Well, let's not disappoint them, a voice whispered from the electrified part of my mind. There's nothing else to do around here.

"Oh, hell no," Boogerilla said, slowing her storming charge to a swaggering stalk. Confident she had her prey cornered and wanting to taunt and tease for the benefit of others. "I be boss bitch around here, you feel me? Real talk. You said all that tough shit while I was behind that door and you felt safe. Now I'm gonna make you hold up for it." She stopped, looked around. "I be BOSS BITCH!" she roared, and, I swear to God, beat her chest while baring her teeth again. She gave several more battle cries, looking around at the other women to make sure she had their attention and were interested in watching the annihilation of this white-bread ho that had challenged her status.

I freaked out, screamed with hands shaking on the sides of my face, pigeon toed, knees bent and saturated in terror, turned and took off running away from the scary giant that would certainly squash me like the pathetic gnat I was. "Nooo! Please don't!" I screamed, my little feet gliding lightly, in perfect balance over the floor.

Boogerilla charged instantly, and rather impressively for a big gal. Like a football linebacker spearing for a tackle she rushed after me. My pretend scared legs must have lost their energy, uh-oh, allowing her to gain in a few seconds. As her heavy steps hammered behind me, one-two-three, I timed them, determined she was up to speed, spun around in a one-eighty pivot, hands up, weight centered, chin down and eyes beaming straight into hers with boiling rage and unshakeable conviction that I would beat her senseless.

Time slowed, megamo, adrenaline hyping senses. She saw me spin around and crouch, my fists, Seek and Destroy, raise in her direction with a look in my eyes that inexplicably zapped the energy she planned to demolish me with. She faltered, her equilibrium wavered, her nervous system too sluggish to do anything about it. Confusion, then realization that she had been tricked crossed her features a split second before she tried and failed to hit the brakes.

But it was way past too late.

"I was just kidding," I told her, shifting my weight forward and to my left, throwing an overhand right from the hip. Like a pitcher winding up to throw a fastball, my arm launched with slingshot action, forearm flexing, fist tightening right as it hit her in the face. Her forward momentum and weight compounded the punch with devastating results. My knuckles crashed into her upper teeth and nose, crushing them. The bridge of bone and cartilage flattened between her eyes, tearing skin, instantly swelling both eyes shut with the trauma. Boogerilla wailed in startled pain as she plowed into my right shoulder and spun to the ground, huge body following an unperceiving head. I pivoted to slip around her. Centered weight on my toes, hands raised for more action. Stepped away from my opponent looking for a neutral corner while the referee did his thing.

"Christ," I said, closing my eyes and shaking my head. "I'm not in a ring. I'm not even a boxer anymore." Looking up, I saw several women looking at me with open mouths.

Laughing and clapping started from nearly every cell, muffled from behind the steel doors but still uproarious enough to make the joint sound like a real fight crowd. One of those things you don't realize how much you miss until you hear it.

I've missed that sound. So bad.

Boogerilla stirred on the floor, mewling wet nasal sounds a person makes when knocked unconscious with a severely broken nose.

I've missed that sound, too. Ah, good times.

Her hands flapped weakly around her head, which was pressed to the floor like a Muslim prostrating herself to Allah, butt in the air, stretched out with arms in the front. A position her body wasn't designed for. It looked painful.

So did the puddle of blood leaking from her nose. I could smell it.

Ouch.

The thought of pain awakened my own. My wrist, numb a second ago, throbbed and shouted at me every curse word in the book.

"Son of a mmm," I said, sucking in a breath and wincing. I grabbed my right wrist, squeezing like that would make it stop aching. It didn't. Opening my eyes, I looked at it. No protruding shards of bone or bulging deformations like my nerves told me were there. I tucked my arm under my boobs, gave Boogerilla another glance then walked back to my cell.

This injury should get me some time off work. Hopefully. Or cost me my job. Likely.

Like I really gave a flying hoo-hah. One punch KO, biatch!

That is what really matters, ladies and gentlemen. Is there a better feeling than when a serious problem is solved, perfectly, according to plan? My wrist screamed bloody murder, but I couldn't think of a more satisfying emotion than the pure ecstasy coursing through my limbs now.

Vivacious, baby.

I walked into my cell and lay down on the bed. Smiling, unable to feel the crude discomfort of the mattress for the floating, drugged euphoria that levitated me into another reality. A sense of peace and sureness asserted itself in my mind. Comfortable thoughts familiar to me in the way a favorite cousin comes home after being away for years, welcomed with open arms by loved ones.

Why did I ever stop doing this? Fighting is in my blood, my first love, and will always and forever be my proudest talent.

The pulsating, rhythmic Feel Good dope tingled in my hair and zinged in my loins. My toes curled, I stretched, groaning in a state of enjoyment that far surpassed the deepest levels of infatuation.

I was in love again. Completely, utterly in love. A fight junkie.

A loud clapping snapped me out of my reverie. I opened my eyes and looked at my cell door, which was closed but not locked. When I figured out the clapping wasn't coming from another cell, I sat up, feet on the floor, and listened to the applauding hands approach.

"Bravo, Cream Tail," Captain Portsmouth said, opening my door, looking in at me. She clapped a few more times, then took a small camcorder from under her arm and waved for me to come to her.

Frowning suspiciously, I stood, walked the six feet to the door. "She started it," I said in an uncaring tone. I crossed my arms and looked at the video camera. Intuition kicked in hard, blaring a warning that a storm was brewing, and it wasn't going to be pretty. No rainbows. It dawned on me that ERT or at least a herd of officers should have rushed in to stop the fight, and maybe even kick us to sleep (or just me, since Boogerilla was already snoozing, hee-hee).

I looked behind her and said, "Um. This may sound odd.

But why aren't I on the floor with a dozen boots upside my head, choking on pepper spray?"

For an answer, she simply smiled. A horrible, slow spreading thing that made horns extend from her already bulging forehead. The cat ate the canary smile. Thunder and lightning should have accompanied that look, ripping and booming above her head. Captain Stormmouth flipped open the camcorder's LCD screen. Powered it on. Pressed playback and waved an invitation for me to view it with her. I admit I was too curious to tell her to go sit on it, so I stepped next to her and hoped I wouldn't catch any flesh eating diseases.

The video showed the zone from the guard tower's perspective. Thirty cells on bottom, thirty up top with a guardrail around the horseshoe-shaped tier. Four steel picnic tables bolted to the dayroom floor, spaced between the cells and the tower. Women looked out of their windows or tray holes.

A cell door on the top tier opened, the lock a faint snick across the cavernous zone. It was my cell, I realized. I came out, glancing around. Took a step forward and froze. Lifted a foot and shook it as if trying to dislodge a dog turd. Looked at my neighbors, shoulders shaking with laughter.

Whoa. I looked goofy. I've never seen a video of myself, other than fight tapes. Reality star material I was not.

The Goofy Me walked toward the stairs and paused as Boogerilla's bellowing voice megaphoned out of her tray slot, heard distinctly inside the tower, sounding just as crude and annoying on a video recording. Worse. I doubt a synthesizer could help that guttural roar. Her titanic head blacked out the entire slot. She stood and the hole blinked with light. Jeepers creepers. The soft click of a lock and her door burst open as she charged straight for the stairs.

Wow. She looked twenty pounds heavier on video. Even managed to look more menacing as she trash-talked her way up the stairs. Our verbal exchange came through the camcorder's speakers in Stereo. Goofy Me morphed into Scared Me. I did my freaked out, backing away from an axe murderer bit, and my opinion of reality show stardom changed.

I was pretty dang good at bringing the drama.

"Like you was really scared, Cream Tail," the captain said, chuckling. "That was mighty fine. I've never seen a fake out like that before, and I've seen a lot of fights."

I looked at the woman and almost started laughing with her. Praise was praise, and people respond to it even when coming from idiots. I looked back at the camera as Boogerilla started her war cries. Captain Portsmouth's chuckle turned into a full laugh, eyes squinting closed, making a face that was hard to look at or listen to. The LCD flopped as her arms shook.

"Her black ass be doing that every time," she said, wheezing and wiping her eyes with her free hand.

"Every time?" I inquired.

She smiled her stormy promise again, thunder and lightning ripping, tumultuous. A tornado following a revelation I wasn't anxious to hear.

On the video, my whole body flipped its wig in terror, turned and ran from a charging beast. Boogerilla gained speed and ground on Scared Me. I suddenly stopped, pivoted, said my badass one-liner while drilling her with an overhand haymaker that smacked loudly into her head. The crunch-wail-shuffling-shoes mix strained the little speakers. Portsmouth and I shared a collective "ooh" and cringed.

I saw and felt the damage that punch did up close. It looked even more gruesome on video. And way cooler, too.

Scared Me was Shocker Me, pivoting away from the falling giant, hands raised, looking for the referee like a dummy. I shook my head, looked away from the camera. My fist throbbed to remind me that scene wasn't fifteen minutes old.

Captain Portsmouth closed the LCD, stuck the camera back under an arm and smiled at me. Hands on hips. Stormy grin. Approaching hurricane status. I steeled myself.

"I want you to fight for me," she said.

Shit! I knew it. I didn't say anything.

This was not happening. Unfreakingbelievable.

"That video was streamed live on the Internet. We have almost a half-million viewers, and we get more with every fight."

"We?"

"We've never had a one-punch KO. Of course, we've never had a professional boxer either."

"Let me get this straight." I unfolded my arms. "You set me up to fight Boogerilla, and made money for whoever 'we' is. And now you expect me to fight for you on a regular basis. Is that right?"

"That's right, Cream Tail. Pretty and smart. You the new star. You just knocked off the champ."

"I don't want it. I don't want any part of this. I've retired from that life," I said, grimacing with reluctance as the words spilled from my lips. *What the fuck is your problem, lady?* screamed a familiar voice in my head. The fight junkie that only moments ago was lying on that bed basking in a multi-orgasmic sea. I tried to quell the wench, the urge, so I could maneuver out of this mess. Working for this broad was a disaster in the making. Hell, I didn't even want to clean the floor on her shift. She kept smiling at me with absolute surety that she would own me, giving me a sinking feeling in my gut.

The fight junkie was jumping up and down in my head, pumping her mental fist with a cheer. *I want to fight! Bring 'em on!*

Crap.

"Oh, I think you do want it, Cream Tail. Everyone has a

price," she said, pulling out a wad of cash from her shirt pocket. Peeling off a hundred dollar bill, she handed it to me. "My girls get a hundred bones a fight. And a fifty dollar bonus if you get a knockout." She peeled off a fifty, dangled it in front of my face.

With a mind of its own, my traitorous hand reached out and took it.

Holding the bills was empowering, a unique rush in its own right. I used to fiend for this stuff. The texture, the smell, of money brought out feelings of success and vivid, positive memories. Images of good times. I haven't even seen money in two years.

But a hundred-and-fifty for one fight? I used to get a hundred times that, more, for that much work. This pocket change wouldn't be worth the wear and tear my body takes training. And my aching wrist certainly suffered more than a bill-fifty in damage.

Reason and plain common sense teamed up on the fight junkie, beating her down and winning a hotly contested battle. Just barely. "I don't want it," I told Portsmouth again. I folded the bills, held them out to her. She just looked at my hand.

Tempestuous smile appearing again, eye of a Category 5, she grabbed the camcorder, powered it on and pointed the lens at me. "Today is March first, two-thousand-and-twelve. Approximately ten-thirty hours. Captain Portsmouth conducting security check. Offender Clarice Carter, J-one-three-three-two, found with major contraband in her possession," she said in a surprisingly clear, professional voice, zooming in on the money in my hand.

I jerked my hands behind my back, stupidly, looking even more guilty for the video. Goofy Me. "Offender refuses to give up the contraband. A take down team will be notified, offender will receive a Rules Violation Report." She closed the camera, smiled at me. The insane bitch even waggled her eyebrows. She didn't need to say anything else.

My wrist pounded harder as my heart switched gears in outrage, telling me it hurt but had no problem sacrificing more if I wanted to drill this yeast infection in her ports mouth. The fight junkie screamed and danced, not caring who she fought for as long as she got to feel the resistance of a human body as she hit it. I suppressed the conflicted opinions and tried to get myself together. I was in real trouble here. That video could get me at least another six months in lockdown, and a mark on my record that could affect my security level. Not conducive to my parole plans.

As my dear husband used to say, I'm an inclined plane wrapped helically around an axis.

Screwed.

"Oh my, Captain. I wonder if you realize how persuasive your charm is. Of course I'll accept your most gracious offer," I said through gritted teeth, eyes narrowed.

She chortled happily, clapping. "I'm glad you came around, Cream Tail. You just remember who be your captain and you'll do okay, hear?"

"Yeah. I hear you."

"Right, then." She turned and walked away.

The eye of the storm moving off, the powerful feeder bands had me in their grasp.

Acknowledgements

MY FIRST novel, *By Hook or Crook*, was a lot of fun to write. It is fast-paced and filled with things that will shock most who read it. I had never studied the craft of writing before, penning it from instinct, yet I've received praise from all who've read it. One guy, an evil genius named Terry Stewart, called it a potential "cult classic." Such positive feedback made me decide to try again, to see if I could write something even better.

I needed to get serious and actually study the art of writing fiction, instead of just reading books and thinking, Hey, I can do that. So I attained some workbooks (thank you Steven Farris) and did the lessons, discovering that I might have a smidgen of natural talent, but had much to improve on. I hope readers will enjoy the added intricacies and changes to my style of writing. I promise to keep studying so future novels will only get better.

I have a limited working knowledge of skills that I can give to my protagonists. Wanting to impress readers, I thought to myself, What's more impressive than a guy who can build cars, box like a pro, and do world-class tattoos? The answer: A girl who can build cars, box, and tatt! Hell yeah. So the star of this story was born, Clarice, a girl extremely talented in everything she does, yet vulnerable, and, I hope, relatable to you wonderful folks who spent your time and money on this book.

I have to thank several people who either helped or provided inspiration for this project. Foremost is my friend, Dennis Newton, who typed this book from my handwritten manuscript (if you just gasped in respect, you are apparently familiar with my handwriting), and put up with the many nit-picking changes I made to the typed version, while adding a thing or two of his own that turned out to be really good ideas. Thank you, D. You have seriously changed my life.

Thanks to my mother, Troie Roy, and my aunt, Wendie Cook, who are nurturing forces that have influenced my life, and are the reason I've maintained good mental health in an environment that promotes the exact opposite. 'Preciate the critique on book #1 and the encouragement on book #2, ladies.

I must thank my friends and test-readers who offered a wide range of perspective on the characters and story: Roy Harper, Thong Le, Trent Eason, and Joseph Jackson.

Special thanks to my boxing trainer, mentor, and very good friend, Fred Williams, who didn't directly help with this project, but whose life and personality inspired the creation of Eddy, Shocker's kickass coach. Old Man, you instilled that spark of ambition in me all those years ago that led to this life-goal achievement. I couldn't have written this without the innumerable physical and mental lessons you challenged me with.

Much love and respect to all of you.

\- Chris Roy
September 13, 2012

About the Author

Chris Roy was born and raised on the Mississippi Gulf with a background in automotive mechanics, tattoo art, and pursues many passions, including boxing and fitness training.

Chris currently resides at the Mississippi State Penitentiary in Parchman. If you would like to correspond with the author, you can send a letter to:

> Chris Roy K8649
> MSP Unit 29
> PO Box 1057
> Parchman, Ms. 38738

NewPulpPress.com

www.ingramcontent.com/pod-product-compliance
Lightning Source LLC
Chambersburg PA
CBHW070515260626
47161CB00004B/1557